THE DOWRY OF VIRGINS
AND
OTHER STORIES

OPHELIA S. LEWIS

VILLAGE TALES PUBLISHING

NORCROSS, GEORGIA

PRAISE FOR THE DOWRY OF VIRGINS

Lewis captures the hearts of her characters in a pleasing poetic style...packed with nourishing nuggets of African parables.

An absolutely delightful collection of stories. You will not even realize that there are lessons to be learned in each one until the end. Lewis weaves a spell that makes each story a page turner, with joy and laughter, tears and sorrow. Her descriptions make you feel as though you are right there with the characters...an excellent way to experience African culture and customs. — C.S. Pierce Artist

Noted for her vividness of description and picturesqueness of diction, in The Dowry of Virgins, Lewis' style is pure and clear. — James Bestman Editor

ALSO BY OPHELIA S. LEWIS

2014 - Dead Gods (HM2)
2013 - **Good Manner Alphabets (*how to be a super polite kid*)
2012 - Montserrado Stories
2011 - Heart Men (a novel)
2009 - **A is For Africa
2009 - **The Good Manners Alphabet Book
2007 - Journeys (a collection of poems)
2004 - My Dear Liberia—Recollections

**Children's Book

Readers of this book are encouraged to contact the author with comments; email *(ophie2020@yahoo.com)* personal website: (*www.ophelialewis. com*), twitter (*@ophie2020*), facebook (*www.facebook.com/ophelia.lewis*)

ISBN:978-0-9753609-2-7
Library of Congress Control Number: 2008934937
Available from Amazon.com and other retail outlets

Available in eBook
eISBN: 978-0-9753609-7-2
Available on Kindle and other devices

Printed in the United States of America

DEDICATION

Because of you, I try.
I love you.
Farah, Lemriel, Nostelda, Duke, Aostelda, Benaelda,
Manseen, Daliette, Sydni, Malik, Razaq, Kaela, and Mylaeka.

ACKNOWLEDGMENTS

I give all the glory to God! And, my tender love to my mother, Jeanette Lewis-Harding, for all her love, support and encouragement.

Aaron, Marie, Veronica, Jenkins (we really miss you), Joann, & Akitee, special thanks and with more gratitude and love than you can ever imagine.

Derick White and Kemberly Harris, thank you for your love and support.

Nadia Assaf-Cole, you've taught me to be a fighter in more ways than you will ever know; love and appreciate you.

My outmost appreciation and thanks to Marilyn Archie, Marilyn Cason, Manseen Logan, Patricia Molloy, Kimberly Moton, and Erica Faulker (my editor), your contributions made this possible.

AUTHOR'S NOTE

The thoughts shared in these stories are intended to entertain. Although the settings are of African (mainly Liberian) themes, no attempt is made to explain a specific ritual of any culture or people from any part of Africa. Their customs are based on bits and pieces of ethnic virtues. It is by my human heart that I gave life to these characters.

In this collection of short stories, themes represented in the work are of African and Liberian cultural influence. It seeks to explore within an African setting the emotions of ordinary people when they face extraordinary situations. The emotions range from love, hate, greed, envy and fear. Lewis placed these ordinary people in unusual situations and let the characters decide for themselves the outcome of the story. In essence, her stories are generally, character-driven. Look for the twist in every tale in this collection!

A New Chief for Gwapala – Egoism lies deep within every man and nothing is impossible to a willing heart. When an astute African chief tests the courage of his men in choosing his predecessor, a hunter, a champion and an entertainer volunteers to explore a precarious forest. Each man returns with a gift, suitable for the throne, but there can only be one chief.

What the Moon Leaves Behind – A grandmother's love is hardly enough for a young woman who has witnessed all the other young women her age become wives. A crippled since birth, Myatu's life was far from ordinary, especially in one of Africa's most prosperous villages where looks and wealth meant everything. Then one day, fate comes in a form of an old man and tests Myatu's heart.

Songs of the Pepper Birds – Necessity knows no law and Kaimu has to confront his pregnant girlfriend's father when he has not engaged her nor has he the means to pay a dowry. Kaimu goes to seek the advice of a wise old man, from whose experience he learns what life can sometimes throw at you—the intense struggle between what is easy and what is right. "A man must give an account of his deeds, no matter how painful," Oldman Jallah tells Kaimu. "Doing the right thing is worth every bit of personal sacrifice."

The Dowry of Virgins – For Josef Yeke, life was pleasant in Twoku Village until an ugly gossip started about his precious daughter that had been defiled. There will be no report of firing gunshots on the night of her wedding to show that she is a virgin. As an important elder, Yeke has the power to sentence the accused to hash punishment, even death. But on the advice of his dearest friend, he must demonstrate forgiveness instead.

Obikai's Heart – Not every African man wishes to partake in the tradition of polygamy, but custom is tyrant. Quonah fell in love with one woman, Obikai, a younger woman promised to Quonah's aged father. Quonah married her anyway. Abandoning tradition is one thing; seeking forgiveness is another. After nine years of separation from his family, Quonah returns to his village to face his dying father and to ask for forgiveness.

Common Threads – The aspiration one has may not always be cheerfully carried, but when your spirit is ready, your feet become light. Caught between her wish to go to school and being forced into an arranged marriage, fourteen year old Aketi must find a new life elsewhere after denying her father his honor—the betroth of one's daughter among their people.

A GLORIOUS PAST
IS
THE WORK OF A GLORIOUS MAN
—African parable—

CONTENTS

A NEW CHIEF FOR GWAPALA

In a former time, but not so long ago that some cannot still re-member, there was a powerful African village nestled deep be-hind the Putu Mountain where the lush stands of virgin African rain forest spread wide towards the great Cavalla River. In fact, this village was the mightiest of all six villages in the region. It was called Gwapala (*y-pa-la*), the untroubled village of reason, ruled by heroic men for four generations after the last stronghold of the slave catchers.

Chief Kojalou inherited Gwapala's leadership from his father when he was still a young man. To celebrate his eighteenth birthday, an oc-casion was arranged to honor the prince, with ceremonies of respect, festivities, and sacrament. During that time, Great Chief Appiija (*i-pee-ja)* placed on his only son's finger a gold ring, symbolizing control of Gwapala's throne. It meant putting in his control a great people, many and strong. This was according to the tradition of the Gwapalians.

Like his father, Chief Kojalou was of note among the people, a mighty man of power. The dread of him was on those tribes hearing his report. He conquered his enemies in every tribal war, fiercely over-powering them and crushing their powerful warriors as would a herd of elephants stomping the forest. Chief Kojalou raised his spears against twelve hundred men, even killing some with their own spears. Those incapable of fighting toe-to-toe with him fled shamefully. Henceforth, his reputation placed on Gwapala the status of Africa's mightiest village.

In spite of the great honor Chief Kojalou had accomplished, he had not fathered a son to take his place and continue his legacy. Granted his daughter, Princess Farah, was a spitting image of him and a photocopy of his personality; even ready and able to lead. But her presence on the throne would only impose costly threats, risking Gwapala's dominant status. The elders brought it to his attention that his daughter was never to become his successor. So Chief Kojalou declared his cause in their ears, he would find Princess Farah a husband suitable to take his place instead.

One week before her nineteenth birthday, a decree was published. There would be no celebrations on the anniversary of the princess' birth, but that every man in Gwapala was to assemble in the [1]palava hut on the eve of her birthday. The town's crier drummed the message continuously for six days, up to the day and time of the meeting. At the precise time, every man of Gwapala heritage hurried to the palava hut to attend the meeting, young and old, wealthy and not so wealthy.

Gathering his people on this day was the high point of Chief Kojalou's guidance. He stood firm and confident before them.

"Sons of our great village, may the winds remain behind your backs!" he greeted the audience.

"Long live our Chief," the people cried their collective responses. They sat attentive.

"These are the best of times," Chief Kojalou started. "I will be careless if I do not remind you of our blessings. A longtime has passed since we fought a tribal war, nights are peaceful and days are promising. The children our wives have bored us, play contently in our yards. Our neighbors respect us as each Gwapalian is an influential man. Even nature has been generous," he chuckled. "Last season rainfall was plenty. Crops fill our stockrooms and the cattle have multiplied fully. My people, do not let it fool you…nothing in life remains the same forever."

The sound of his voice honorably carried his father's legacy. His words were pleasing to their listening ears, they nodded their heads, approving. The aged councilors, of title and authority, sat swollen with pride, seeing the great Chief Appiija in the image of his son.

"In a man's life, time is of the essence," Chief Kojalou continued. "No matter what great thing a man does, it has to pass. Like my father, the Great Chief Appiija, I too, have grown old. I do not vainly

---

1 *In many parts of Africa, the Palava hut is the largest hut in the village that is used for the town meeting place. High-carved posts support its palm-thatch roof and the wall is only waist high so those standing outside can see and hear as well as those seated inside. Everyone attending the meeting is able to involve himself or herself and no one is left out*

wish that my days should go on forever and I do not know for how long I will be with you. When I'm no longer with you, it is important that Gwapala carry on the status of greatness. As my father did, so must I. I, too, must pass control to my heir."

Mumbling noise erupted in the assembly at once. They argued the princess would not be able to continue his heir.

"I know that Princess Farah cannot assume such duty being a woman," Chief Kojalou said, calming the noise. "I also know that an outsider cannot become heir to my throne. With that in mind, I must choose among you a man who is to marry my daughter. Nevertheless, he must earn this honor and prove worthy of the task."

"What then is asked of a man to prove worthy of this task?" One councilor asked.

"He who travels five hundred miles toward the great river," Chief Kojalou replied.

The audience moaned louder, aware of the great risk.

"Who are you going to choose?" Another councilor asked.

"I will not choose among you," Chief Kojalou said. "I cannot send a man into such danger for my own need. He is to take on this challenge at will. He must travel the jungle for three days and return with an object suitable to show his courage."

Silence took over the palava hut. The challenge was precise as it was critical. Every sniffle was heard. The men sat as lifeless statues. One would have easily been startled by the sound as light as falling feathers. Never had anyone dared venture more than three hundred miles outside the region. The forest had an intimidating history of extraordinary tales and terrifying unnatural dealings. It had been proven, time and again, mercy had never been shown to want-to-be heroes.

Everyone remembered Ijoba (*e-jo-ba*), the jungle's newest victim. Ijoba was one of Gwapala's finest warriors who fought side by side with Chief Kojalou in many of their tribal wars. He raised his own spear against eight hundred men. Nevertheless, a few days ago in his old age, Ijoba left Gwapala against his family's wish to wander the mysterious jungle alone. After a week of his troublesome absence, rumors started that it would be impossible for Ijoba to make it back home.

The men began debating with one another in low urgings, discussing their honorable times of the past and the importance of their future.

Suddenly, the robust body of one Owozu stood and every head twisted toward him. He was their current wrestling champion, known as *Jungle Cat* because his back had never touched the earth. Owozu was unmatched in fifty-two fights every year. He had kept the title for more than fifteen years, clearly beating his opponents and giving in to their begging submissions. Standing six feet and eleven inches tall, his presence was commanding and as intimidating as his husky voice. His frame was upheld by his heavy build, a godlike man with a chest as broad as the base of a mango tree. Furrowing his brow, his face expressed his deepest thoughts.

Simbonga stood tall immediately, sporting his beefy chest and well-defined washboard torso. The daisy chain of snake skulls hanging around his thick neck, rattled. Also encircling his waist was his ²*juju*, a string made of several tiny skulls which swung back and forth with the slightest movement of his body. Simbonga claimed they were the skulls of unborn baby leopards. No one questioned this brave hunter because of his perfect hunting past.

A hunter such as Simbonga had high ranking and to a hunter, tracking an animal is like dancing; it makes his body happy. The best hunters chase their game, but may leave it if the animal is too fast. To them, it was not meant to be. Simbonga, on the other hand, would risk death in his manner of hunting. He knew all the places the animals hid, every den and every hole. Any animal that Simbonga met was meant for him. He chased his game to its death. There had never been a time when he returned from his hunting trip empty-handed. Besides, not once had his big game been matched with any other hunter's game. Even his father, whose closeness with Simbonga made them best friends, never understood the magic of his skills.

As they waited for more volunteers, to their surprise, a third man stood; but to mumbling skepticism, realizing who he was. Many might have assumed correctly if Kudah was excusing himself from the meeting. It was quiet shocking to see him taking on the challenge—an entertainer had no business in such competition. Kudah's lips were twenty percent more plumply than the average Gwapalian's lips and he spoke his words sluggishly. But his voice was as musical

---

2 *Magical power, usually having to do with spirits or luck, which is bound to a specific object*

as any instrument, in a pleasant way. The audience was moved to inspiring psalms whenever he sang and plucked the strings on his handmade guitar.

Kudah waited with the others.

Moments went by and no one else stood. It turned out just the three men were willing to try. Soon soft pleas turned into muffled arguments. Chief Kojalou raised his hand, waved his elephant-tailed switch and the noise stopped.

"You, three men, must begin your journey at once," he gave his order immediately. "You may explore caves in the forests; search the rivers and mountaintops. Seek anything mystical…perhaps extraordinary, to prove your courage. May the God of the earth walk before each of you."

Chief Kojalou finished and marched out of the palava hut and then back to his hut. The elders and councilors quietly followed. In a little while, the men disassembled and went strolling quietly back to their individual homes.

At sundown, Gwapala had that same soft delicate texturing of the evening found in most African villages. With the smell of firewood burning under the evening meals, cooking fires discharged trails of dusky blue smoke far across the sky. Family members declared the men fearful send-offs as many of the women purposely held back tears since they were too scared to bring any bad luck on the travelers. Their usual social gatherings extended until late evening because of the forthcoming event. Then at dawn, the three men left Gwapala and begun their hike towards the Cavalla River.

When tension mounts too high in a village, it is the drums that bring people back to themselves and they become calm once more. During the time of the men's absence, the talking drums rumbled day and night. Life continued normally but with reasonable amounts of reluctance. The women did their usual fishing at the nearby creek. Some men plowed their farms while others looked after their herds. The children played games in the yard throughout the day. Then at sundown, many sat around the hearth in their [3]kitchens to hear folktales told by the old people about legends of their time.

Sunrise on the fourth day was barely visible when every occupier

---

3 A small wall-less shed, usually next to the family hut, where food is prepared; guests are also entertained there.

of Gwapala woke up. With the day's work suspended, each adult man rushed to the palava hut carrying his own wooden bench or sitting mat to get the perfect viewing post. The palava hut grew crowded from one end to the other as every available space was quickly taken. There were as many men standing outside as there were men sitting inside. Boys too young to attend the meeting, but mature enough to use a [4]*cutlass*, were told to cut fresh palm branches for decorations. Apprentices of winemakers were ordered to fill large wooden barrels with the finest [5]*palm wine*. The women started the food preparation, as edibles of every kind were subjected to boiling, frying, and roasting. Young women involved themselves with dancing to the old [6]*Zoë's* rattling [7]*sasa*, skillfully matching the rumbling drums.

By noon, the entire village was wrapped in beautiful fresh green palm branches. Chief Kojalou had entered the palava hut before all and had already taken his seat on the sculptured ivory throne. Elders and councilors took their places on both sides of him, honorably dressed in colors according to their ranks. Each man held in his hand either a lion-tailed, leopard-tailed, or a tiger-tailed switch, showing individual accomplishments. The men waited patiently to hear the words that were to weave the tales of the travelers' journey.

Arrayed in an extravagant royal blue garment, Chief Kojalou rose majestically to high applauding hands and stomping feet. His robe hung handsomely down to his ankles. On it were hand-embroidered patterns in elaborate bright gold thread. The matching trousers fit tight at his ankles, slightly above diamond-covered sandals covering his feet. He raised his elephant-tailed switch, the drums stopped.

"Let the forum begin!" Chief Kojalou called the meeting to order and took his place back on the ivory throne.

From the back of the palava hut, Simbonga's six-foot-nine body moved forward with poise. Drawing his load behind his heels, he advanced with heavy steps, thumping the palava hut stridently. Every muscle in him gathered, steadily swinging him forward. He reached

---

4 *A large, heavy-bladed knife used for cutting down dense underbrush.*

5 *The sap of the palm tree which trickles into a gourd and ferments into wine*

6 *(pronounced 'zoo' with an o sound) The medicine woman who dispenses medicines and controls the spirit-filled aspects of community life*

7 *Musical instructions made by threading beads, seeds, or shells on strings, which cradled the whole gourd (dried, hollowed-out shell of an ornamental fruit). As the strings are jerked, the seeds snap against the gourds, making a cha-cha sound.*

the front, released the sack from his shoulder, and dumped his load on the ground. Simbonga bowed his face and greeted the chief and elders. Then, he turned to the audience and greeted them, also with a bow.

"Look at my feet," Simbonga bragged, lifting one foot, then the other. The audience grunted at the sighting of rasping blisters. "Are they not witnesses to the distance I've traveled?"

They applauded more praises for Simbonga.

"Show us what you've brought," Chief Kojalou said, as if challenging.

"Great Chief, you asked that we travel five hundred miles into the great jungle, is it not so?"

Chief Kojalou nodded 'Yes'.

"I traveled six hundred miles instead!"

The audience bellowed to Simbonga's claim. A six-hundred mile journey into the jungle was astonishing.

"When I reached the Cavalla River, I had not found a suitable entity to prove my courage, so I decided to go beyond it," Simbonga defended his claim. "You have heard tales of this great river, but only a few men have seen it. For those whom the Cavalla will remain a tale, embrace your hearts. I speak the truth today, when I tell you, the Cavalla River is the god of all rivers! As far as my eyes could see, it seemed stretched to the end of the earth."

This report wooed the crowd, the men applauded more. They continued until Chief Kojalou waved his switch to move the presentation along.

"A strange thing happened," Simbonga warned as he continued his tale. "I saw an old man sitting by the river's brink. I asked him, why he was there; he babbled of being ill and begged me to gather him some herbs. What was I to do? I had not traveled into the jungle to waste my time with an old man. I told him the purpose of my journey and hurried to search for my object to prove my courage.

"I searched the river's edge for a canoe but did not find one, so I jumped in the giant river and swam across it. It took me forty-five minutes to swim across. What I witnessed beyond the great river has no comparison to any other," Simbonga bragged. "The animals were monstrous! The lions are as big as the elephants we see around these parts and their roars echo far, even deafening to my ears. The elephant that I saw had a shadow that covered the grounds of one hut standing on top of another. I stood amazed at such discovery and decided to kill two lions and one elephant to bring them back as my findings."

An enthusiastic outburst of applause erupted to Simbonga's claim, an [8]*elephant killer*. For four generations, only Chief Kojalou and Chief Appiija had held that title. Great Chief Appiija was buried with all his elephant spoils, at his request, so his son earned his own. Chief Kojalou earned his own spoil, which he wore on each arm daily; twenty bracelets made from the elephant's hard toe-skin. The five elephant-tailed switches, each encased with fine leather handles, were his five badges of honor. One accompanied him always, interchanging them with his official visits. Somehow, Simbonga's claim was not hard on the dignity of the chief. A respectable hunter, such as Simbonga, would make a good replacement.

Simbonga unsealed the sack and freed its contents with a thunderous plop. The crowd stood and roared in amazement, their eyes froze in stares. Two tusks from the elephant were laying almost six-foot along beside each other and the lions' heads resembled giant oak stumps. Simbonga's discoveries were strikingly grand, to say the least.

"I have brought enough ivory to make a new throne for our Chief," Simbonga boasted. "And the heads of these lions," he pointed, "are sure to prove Gwapala is more powerful than it is already known."

Chief Kojalou nodded with pride, showing obvious admiration for the hunter's parcel. The old chief seemed satisfied, which made Simbonga happy. The elephant killer stepped to the side and made

---

8 *Of all the hunters, an elephant killer is an extraordinary man. First, he strips himself down to a loincloth, carefully covering his entire body with oil. The hunter carries three spears and the burden of these carefully chiseled iron-headed tools is, without a doubt, a boost to his ego. Armed with them, he crawls through the jungle towards a grazing herd of elephants that he has tracked down and followed for many days. Creeping up behind the nearest monster, he places his body with the choicest spear, within two or three feet of the animal. The javelin shooter lets go of his spear and runs. Usually the elephant dashes off madly and it is on this action the hunter's life depends. The wounded elephant, with the spear shot halfway through his heart, will sometimes wander about for several days before he dies, all the time being patiently trailed by the hunter. Failing to kill an elephant, all which is left of the hunter, is a gory spot in the earth where the elephant trampled him. There has been evidence of those failing to such task. On many occasions, they have found abandoned spears that have been twisted into corkscrew looking metals by the wounded monster.*

way for the next traveler.

Owozu marched to the front hauling one hefty bag over each of his broad shoulders. His stride became more powerful to their eager handclaps. He reached the front, easily tossed both bags to the ground and greeted Chief Kojalou and the elders with a slight bow. Then he turned to the assembly. They cheered their hero as if he'd won another title.

"You should begin," Chief Kojalou said, challenging the prized fighter.

"Great Chief," Owozu bowed, "I walked further than Simbonga did...seven hundred miles, to be exact."

As the crowd applauded, Chief Kojalou urged him to continue.

"The Cavalla is the greatest river," Owozu confirmed Simbonga's story about the Cavalla River. "However, the size did not bother me. I also met the old man, but I gave him the brush-off. Then after easily crossing the river, I entered the jungle and saw Simbonga's so-called beasts. The animals seemed great in the eyes of ordinary men, not to me...only prompted me to travel farther. I walked until I reached the land of the Zamzummims."

The Zamzummims, Chief Kojalou thought, even he had not met them face-to-face. The audience grasped Owozu's tale and urged for more, having heard about the giants. Men look like grasshoppers in the sight of these great men of status.

"Yes, the Zamzummims," Owozu declared. "And, today I will not leave you ignorant of the facts. I also found gold in their land, which in fact, is the shrine of might."

"Tell us more," Chief Kojalou cheered.

"To own a piece of gold, you must take part in a brutal contest," Owozu exclaimed. "My comrades, make sure that you're the greatest fighter of all, because strength is measured against strength...like the beats of a running-man's heart. As you fight, pounding the earth with heavy foot-stomps, the men groan of energy echo like thunder. The match is gruesome as contenders fight to the death and you attack your opponents like an exceptionally schooled warrior. Some men lose their limbs, others, their ears. I ripped a man's nose off his face and witnessed another man dig out the eyes of his opponent. One must be brutal, because the match only ends when one man is left standing, and that man is awarded the gold. Do not think greed commits a man to such logic, it is his pride," Owozu said smiling.

"This is an extraordinary report," an Elder mumbled.

"Indeed," Chief Kojalou agreed, "Go on, Owozu, go on."

"Yes, the strife was fierce," Owozu continued. "I fought in three matches and not once did my back touch the earth. I suffered no injury, just minor scratches from their desperate attempts to escape my holds. My strength made my steps bigger…my feet were like an elephant's feet. I did not slip, but chased my opponents down and destroyed them. And as they fell, I stomped them into dwellers of the dust. At the end of three fights I had collected two bags of gold and thought of fighting for more, but the third day was approaching and I had to return to Gwapala."

"Show us the gold," an elder requested.

Owozu unlaced the two bags and tipped both over, spilling gold nuggets over the ground. Those sitting in the back, without good view, hurriedly shifted their positions, stretching their necks to see.

"The hunter's gifts can be used to decorate Chief Kojalou's new treasure hut," Owozu teased.

Laughing broke out. Chief Kojalou nodded a lighthearted reproach at Owozu, who nodded his regret politely. Then he left the front to join Simbonga.

Kudah walked unhurriedly into the palava hut with his arms close to his body, hiding a small bag in his fist. He reached the front and stood studying the audience, as if in a trance.

"What have you brought?" Chief Kojalou challenged.

"It is by you, Chief Kojalou, that we enjoy this great quietness in our region," Kudah began. "Every worthy deed that is done in Gwapala is by your influence. And, I accept it always, most noble Chief, with thankfulness. I hope you and my comrades will accept my humble words, as God is my witness, what I say to you is true."

"Go on," Chief Kojalou said.

Kudah collected his thoughts before continuing.

"I do not know what had inspired me to take on this task, perhaps I did not think it through," he confessed. "On the day of my journey, I stood at the edge of the village for three hours. I hesitated, pressed hard to turn back. I was reluctant to move forward, being stuck in the quicksand of fear. Then I gathered the memory of my grandmother into a bundle of courage and started walking.

"My feet ached with every step, but I refused to turn back. Grand-mother taught me, a man is nothing if his promises are not honored and the proportions of his challenge are always manageable. But, he must try at his best, even if it means losing his life. I had to honor my promise."

Chief Kojalou nodded to Kudah's concept.

"I cannot boast of my gift," Kudah continued, "because I did not search for it…it found me."

"How so," Chief Kojalou asked.

"The old man, whom I met at the river, gave it to me," Kudah said. "When I reached the river, amazed by the size of it, I had not seen the old man until he called out to me. He seemed troubled. I hurried my steps toward him and asked why he'd come to the river. He told me he had come to gather herbs, but had injured his foot and was unable to return home. When I told the old man the purpose of my search, he told me that Owozu and Simbonga had since been and gone. I pondered the matter seriously; if I helped the old man, it would further slow my progress and I would have no time for catching up. Then again, I could not have abandoned an old man who was incapable of defending himself…if an animal attacked him. I made a decision quickly…to abandon the contest.

Chief Kojalou grunted.

"I gathered herbs, according to the old man's instructions, and prepared his medicine," Kudah continued. "I quickly wrapped his foot in it. As I prepared to return to Gwapala, the old man handed me a small pouch. He suggested I present it as my finding, with a strong caution–I was not to open the bag, under no circumstance. With a great deal of reasoning between us, I accepted his gift and returned to Gwapala."

Kudah held the pouch high for the audience to see, and then he handed it to Chief Kojalou. Chief Kojalou received the pouch and Kudah joined the other travelers.

Based on the men's findings, many could not choose a winner. Some argued that Simbonga's enormous animals were grand, even dazzling. Yet others insisted the gold Owozu had brought would take Gwapala's prosperity to greater status. For a lifetime, no other village in the region would be able to match their wealth. Furthermore, Ku-dah's small pouch held a troubling mystery.

While the audience sat eagerly, waiting for Chief Kojalou to deliver his ruling, he studied the audience, then the three travelers.

"I have decided on whose shoulders, the crown would be placed," Chief Kojalou said finally. "But first, let it be known, nothing would be greater than the deeds of these three men." He pointed at Simbonga, Owozu, and Kudah.

The assembly erupted with cheers.

Chief Kojalou waved his elephant-tail switch for silence, but to no use. Their rallying cheers continued.

Without warning, Chief Kojalou drew in his breath and cried, "Ijobaaaaaaaaaaaaaaa...show your face!"

The audience gasped to Ijoba's sudden appearance, stunting the crowd. Holding a spear in his left hand and a glistening machete in his right, he charged into the palava hut carrying his leopard-tail switch locked between his lips. Ijoba marched like a lad eager for manhood, rather than a man stricken with age. The white chalk masking, covering his upper body and face, had not a speck of perspiration disturbing it. Many argued that it was Ijoba's ghost. Some men blamed the palm-wine they had drunk for three whole days. Ijoba's three brothers, sitting at the back of the crowd, stood with the state of unconsciousness. They did not know whether to embrace him or run out of the palava hut.

Ijoba put down his gears and stood before Chief Kojalou, upright. Chief Kojalou pulled the strings sealing the pouch Kudah had given him, and pried it open. Then, he held it out to Ijoba. Ijoba jammed his hand into it, pulled out a metal-liked thing and lifted his hand high above his head. Every man in the audience recognized the gold ring between Ijoba's two fingers.

Murmurs quickly changed into bashing arguments, seeing the ring belonged to Chief Kojalou, the one his father had given him. Some men accused Kudah of stealing Gwapala's honor. Others defended his innocence, recounting his good character. The elders and councilors hung their heads, as disrespect rested heavily on their hearts. Even Kudah began trembling and could not achieve calmness no matter how hard he tried. His entity simply screamed crude disloyalty. Worst, it would not be possible to remove such disgrace brought on his family's good name.

"The ring was not stolen," Chief Kojalou cautioned without delay and reclaimed the ring from Ijoba's hand.

The elders and councilors lifted their heads, and then arguments subsided, momentarily, to undertone complaints.

"Chief Kojalou, you must share your knowledge of it quickly," one councilor requested.

"Yes, I will," Chief Kojalou replied and started at the beginning, telling them about his meeting with Ijoba. He'd sent for Ijoba to ask for counsel, choosing a new chief for Gwapala, but Ijoba had politely refused. So he convinced him that even a great chief cannot think of everything and he needed his help. For seven days and seven nights, he and Ijoba counseled each other, combining logic and reasoning. Finally, they agreed that Ijoba would pose as a helpless old man to test the heart of the travelers. Although dangerous, the plan seemed pleasing. Ijoba accepted the challenge for his people, taking the ring with him into the cruel forest.

Chief Kojalou finished and walked to where the travelers were standing.

"Listen keenly," he said to the men. "Today, I share with you the power of wisdom which was given to me by my father...it has been the key to good judgment."

Simbonga, Owozu, and Kudah nodded.

"Many nights, when most were deep in their sleep, I sat on a mat near my father's bed," Chief Kojalou continued. "He taught me many things...mostly counsel of our fathers. First, a man must praise God for the power that is given to him because no one gets it on his own. Power is not given for self-proclamation; it is given for consciousness sake. If you fail to praise God for it, you are certain to do evil with it."

Then Chief Kojalou tuned to the audience.

"Do not think of yourself more than you ought to think," he said. "God has given to each man the measure of his heart. You will sometimes see situations as lines that never meet...it is because only God can see every situation in its entirety."

"Yes, it is only, God," an old elder repeated.

"You must try hard at being kind, rather than being right," Chief Kojalou continued. "Remember, you cannot always be right, but you can always be kind. The acts of kindness never turn mighty men into fainthearted beings."

Then Chief Kojalou turned toward the travelers.

"Each of you saw the old man sitting by the riverbank, but some did not recognize his needs," he said. "He begged for your help, yet some did not hear him. It was because you did not use your heart. Today, you may seem like righteous heroes in the eyes of your brothers, how will they see you tomorrow?"

Owozu hung his head.

"It is not up to you to predict your future," Chief Kojalou continued. "A man does not have control on his future, or how he is to be. It is only God who sees the future and has control of it. When your heart pulls you in one direction and your head tells you something else, put emphasis on your heart. Always remember, men look at your performance, but God weighs your heart."

Chief Kojalou walked away from the travelers and turned toward the audience.

"Do not forget the things I tell you today," he said. "As long as you live, do not let them slip from your heart. Teach them to your children and they, too, will teach it to their children. Yesterday, our fathers owned Gwapala. Today, Gwapala is no longer for our fathers; the village belongs to us...tomorrow, it will be our children's.

"Honor your brother as you honor yourself...never walk in strife or envy, always walk honestly. And, put no obstacle in your brother's way just to gain power. Do not look down on him who owns far less than you, rather, let him have part of what is yours. When a man pays kindness to another, he paves the way for his own good fortune.

"Search for your brother when he is lost...hold him when he is straggling...look after him when he is sick and bandage his hurt. Do not live by yourself or you will die by yourself. Encourage each other...build each other up, as our fathers have done in the past. Finally, my sons, each of you must always be another's helper."

Sound fell away in the palava hut, like the calmness of early dawn, as Chief Kojalou completed his proverbial preaching.

"Chief Kojalou, whom have you chosen?" an old elder asked.

"It is, Kudah," Chief Kojalou announced.

"Kudah?" the old elder asked.

A unified grunt exploded in the audience. It was neither annoyance nor contempt, just more of a surprise. Kudah went from leaning, seemingly worn-out from his journey, to standing. Simbonga's shoulders dropped, he'd failed to satisfy his hope and expectations.

Owozu sighed, still feeding his ego with an unduly high opinion of himself. His first defeat, in any competition, seemed as clear as day.

"I have prepared the road on which Kudah is to follow," Chief Kojalou said. "It will not be different for him. Our people have always held together in the past. You will be loyal to him as you have been to me."

Chief Kojalou then took hold of Kudah's right hand and said, "My son, when you rule Gwapala after me, put your trust in God's hands, and not your own. Whatever you will accomplish, it will come from God. Allow your heart to follow the judgments of our fathers… and the elders…and the councilors. You will prosper in everything that you do. Take heed to their words and let your deeds be done always in truth. Kudah, you will not fail…no man has ever sat on Gwapala's throne and failed. Always remember, a leader must have eyes to recognize the needs of others, he must have hands to serve others and a heart to share with others the good things in life. Follow the rules that have been followed from the past–never share the [9]blood of war during peacetime. Finally, always show kindness to the poor and to strangers."

Chief Kojalou opened Kudah's hand and placed the gold ring in it. Kudah accepted the ring and immediately dressed Chief Kojalou's finger with it. Then, he raised the old chief's hand and waved the audience to stand. From the back of the palava hut, one man lifted his voice in raising their battle song. Then, the rest of the men lifted their voices, harmonious, hoarse, and harsh. They sang their sacred song like they did after winning each tribal war.

The men rejoined the rest of the people and an extravagant celebration was started; the women had prepared food in abundance. Palm-wine was served out of large [10]*calabashes* and consumed as fast as the wine barrels were refilled. The festivities continued all day and lasted through the night. When daylight took over, except for the two-hundred guardsmen that remained alert always for the safety of the village, everyone had celebrated beyond exhaustion.

Two months passed, then lavish celebration was arranged for Kudah and Farah's wedding. However, it was not until after Chief

---

9 *To take the life of an enemy revengefully, using one's power or status, long after a settlement has been granted*

10 *The dried hollow shell of a gourd used as a bowl, cup, etc.*

Kojalou's death, Kudah became Gwapala's new chief. Until that time, as promised, Chief Kojalou molded the entertainer into a fearless warrior, training him in all manners of warfare. He awarded Kudah with his twenty bracelets and the gold ring. The five elephant-tailed switches were placed next to Chief Kojalou's body at the bottom of his grave, as ordered by Kudah.

Gwapala remained dominant and there was peace in Gwapala all the days of Kudah's ruling. Provisions were made for everyone, rich as well as poor, the people lacked nothing.

KINDNESS BEGETS KINDNESS
—African parable—

WHAT THE MOON LEAVES BEHIND

In those days when the people of Monomono Village flourished with the goodness of nature--plenty of rain, sunny days, mineral wealth, and happiness--they dealt snobbishly with those less fortunate. This small village developed more wealth than most because of its skillful farmers, artisans, and brilliant traders. Monomono Village also owned the famously supreme Botota Market which drew people from all over the province for their livelihood.

African markets are famous for their magnificent goods, but none more so than Botota Market. If you are not lucky to visit Botota Market, you can only imagine the scenery with jealousy for those who have. The crowd is packed solid. People have to dodge and weave to make any progress, threading their way pass bustling stalls and the multitude of shoppers. One seller will persuade you to buy from her piled-high dried fish or butchered cows and goats, while another will show you cooking pots and pans. Stacked apparel of indigo-dyed shirts, country cloth, and shining batik lappas are suspended slightly above flashy jewels, tools, and medicines. Your field of vision is almost confusing, seeing the many different objects, patterns, and colors.

On top of that, a special event takes place every second Wednesday of each month. Ethnic dancers from all parts of Africa come to compete for a title called Africa's Finest Dancer, the popular acknowledgment of a chosen few who have earned the right to great admiration. Enormous esteem is shown for the winner in praise, tributes, and fame.

Traditionally, when strangers in Africa pass through a village, they are invited to rest and food and water is offered to them. However, the people in Monomono Village never cared to help anyone, especially poor strangers. It was different in Sayuwoe's (*sa-u-woo*) case, being an outsider who had made her home there. Sayuwoe was a basket maker with a good report of all who lived in Monomono Village. Her clients included influential elders and other nobles who came from afar. But, Sayuwoe did not limit sales to just them. She also designed baskets for those who had no means of paying her. Next to her hut was an open shed where she and Myatu, her granddaughter, bent and wove colorful ¹*elephant grass* into beautiful baskets. They stained these baskets in different shades and colors, giving them rare characteristics and beauty and then Sayuwoe sold her baskets at Botota Market.

After her husband, Tekoa (*te-ko-i*), died in a hunting accident, Sayuwoe moved to Monomono Village. One unfortunate night, all that was left of the hunter's body was a gory spot where an elephant had trampled him. Sayuwoe lamented for a year, refusing food and turning down invitations to all social engagements. Her life went lower than her surroundings, almost to her own death, to the point where she could no longer remain in Gwapala. Finally, in need of change, Sayuwoe packed her belongings and bid her family farewell. She moved to Monomono Village with their daughter, Liopu (*le-o-poo*), her sole purpose for living.

Her daughter grew up from a cute little girl into a beautiful woman. Liopu's eyes twinkled like the sunshine and her lips were neither thick nor heavy. Her mouth always opened with a pleasant smile, disclosing the tiny gap between her teeth. Most men found it enticing and so Liopu attracted many suitors, famous and not so famous. Of all those suitors, Gbarzon (*ba-zon*) was whom Sayuwoe picked for her granddaughter.

Although he belonged to a family of some rank, Gbarzon's care for others went beyond his own. When one hundred dollars was a strenuous amount for most men, Gbarzon's family willingly offered a generous ²*dowry* value of five hundred dollars. The dowry was made of two cows, five large goats, twenty-five white hens, ten roosters, three 100-pound bags of rice, and two 100-gallon drums of palm oil. Gbarzon married Liopu in a lavish celebration in front of more than three hundred relatives and guests. After the ceremony, the bride and groom were awarded the inheritance of Gbarzon's father's prosper-

---

1 *The heavy grass grows in the savannas of Africa, along lakebeds and rivers, where the soil is rich. It is used to tightly weave baskets, making them strong and flexible*

2 *To betroth a daughter - A contract by means of payment; made by a man for a young girl (virgin) in becoming his wife. The parents or guardian is obligated to uphold the contract*

ous rice business.

To Sayuwoe's liking, the couple lived in walking distance; making it possible for Liopu to come to her mother's hut to weave baskets while Gbarzon tended the daily operations of his business. One morning Liopu entered her mother's kitchen beaming like the early morning sun. Before Sayuwoe could ask the reason behind her daughter's pleasing appearance, Liopu announced the news; the couple was expecting their first child. Sayuwoe danced to a made-up song, promising the child would lack nothing.

The following day Sayuwoe gathered all the bamboo and elephant grass she would need to make a basket, abounding in beauty. She patterned the basket with intricate designs, layered in folds that one could not easily interpret. Then she stained it with a special dye which gave it its dramatic red coloring. Everyone who saw the basket asked to buy it, offering unusually large sums of money. Sayuwoe refused, telling them the basket was for her daughter's unborn child. She was not willing to sell it for any amount of money.

Except for one or two isolated instances, Liopu carried the pregnancy with little discomfort. It was only her unusual craving of rice cooked in coconut milk, which Gbarzon fed her happily. He cooked the food himself, and often joked that cooking was easy so he did not understand why women made an issue of it.

Every morning Sayuwoe met Liopu at her door and waited blissfully to hear about the baby's kick or how well Gbarzon cooked the rice the day before. He had never cooked it right, but boasted often that he did. So her husband does not look bad, Liopu always lied the rice grains were fluffy. But Sayuwoe knew better. When Liopu finished her report, the two women rolled with laughter at Gbarzon's expense.

One morning when Liopu did not show up, Sayuwoe went to check on her daughter because the days were not yet concluded for her to be delivered. She met Gbarzon trying his best to make his wife comfortable, but failing in his efforts. Even with his petting, Liopu refused Gbarzon's rice. She only sipped some of the water Sayuwoe force-fed her.

"You should have come to get me! Go now and call [3]*Zoë* Cheyae

---

3 *(pronounce like 'zoo' but with an o sound) The medicine woman who dispenses medicines and controls the spirit-filled aspects of community life in the village*

(*ch-a-yee*)!" Sayuwoe shouted at Gbarzon.

Gbarzon bounded out the door and ran as fast as his feet could carry him, straight to the midwife's hut. The two returned and Cheyae began medical interventions.

The evening breeze was different in the middle of the scorching dry season, crisp and pleasingly blowing. Sayuwoe opened the bedroom window to fill the room with fresh air, thinking perhaps the full moon will spark relief for Liopu's labor pains. But Liopu's pain worsened as daylight faded into deep nightshade. She suffered the entire evening, moaning in tears. Then, more critical complications developed–the baby had turned sideways in Liopu's belly.

Cheyae advised her patient the baby's legs had to be disjointed to make delivery possible. Nevertheless, Liopu pleaded in tears for the unborn child, stating that she would rather die than allow such cruelty done to her baby. After a great deal of reasoning, Sayuwoe persuaded her daughter to consider Cheyae's advice. She was to consider her own life, not just the baby. Convinced the baby would heal, Liopu reluctantly agreed.

After many difficult maneuverings, strategically separating the unborn baby's knee joint as well as her ankle, Cheyae helped Liopu deliver her child. Sayuwoe was so happy that she wept at the sound of her granddaughter's first cry. She even named the baby, Myatu (*me-i-too*), after her grandmother. Myatu's cry sounded simple, but knowing that Liopu's fight seemingly looked hopeless, her cry was as if she was begging for her own mother's arm. All the pampering Sayuwoe gave the child did not keep her from crying.

Liopu's condition worsened. Pale skin, rapid pulse beat, and dizziness confirmed hemorrhaging. For more than thirty-five years Cheyae had helped many women deliver their babies, and without losing a single person, but the skillful practitioner could not help Sayuwoe's daughter. Exhaustion took over Liopu's body. She slipped into an everlasting sleep, spinning the mood in Gbarzon's home with weeping until morning.

Everyone knew how much Gbarzon loved his wife, even more than life itself. All expected him to grieve, but Gbarzon's grief went beyond measure. He wept publicly, when most men would deny even weeping at any time. Heavy drinking caused him to develop an abnormal craving for alcohol, to the point where not a sober day was left in him. Gbarzon neglected his farmwork, ignored important details of his business, spent all his profits on alcoholic drinks, and eventually ran out of money. Borrowing money from relatives and friends, which he could not repay, spoiled his good name and killed his relationships. Finally, Gbarzon lost his rice business because of the debts, leaving the support of the family solely on Sayuwoe. Because of his shame, he left his village one day to return no more.

The baby grew with a striking resemblance of Liopu, but life was not easy for her. Myatu's legs did not heal properly, leaving one leg shorter than the other. She moved unsteadily, from side to side, to keep her balance. The children in the village chased Myatu at every chance, forcing her to run. When she fell, they mocked her and laughed. Myatu was unable to make friends. Because of this, she spent all of her time in the company of her grandmother and Sayuwoe's love propelled her into managing.

Myatu mastered basket weaving better than her mother and grandmother. Her designs were far better looking than Sayuwoe's baskets even though Sayuwoe had more experience. Myatu enjoyed creating better designs, but hearing stories about relatives seemed more enjoyable. The only thing troubling was Sayuwoe's deliberate cunningness to leave Gbarzon completely out of the stories. When reminded of it, Sayuwoe simply changed to a different topic.

During the raining season, the evening breeze over Monomono Village is usually delightful and is most appreciated at dusk. People are transformed into soft-spoken beings, from the blue in the cooking smoke, which softness seems the color of their thoughts. Everyone gathers with family to share events of the day.

One evening after dinner, after all the dishes were cleaned, except for the pot with the leftovers sitting beside the dim burning charcoals; Sayuwoe joined Myatu in their kitchen to relax. Sayuwoe was talking in guarded utterance about her hopes for a profitable sale the following day, when a sudden release of cruel taunting disrupted the quiet village. A small group of boys, mostly teenagers, were giving chase to an old man dressed in rags. They threw sticks at him while shouting, "Go away, you old beggar! Go away!" While most of their aims were off target, the old man, far advance in years and not fast enough, caught a stick near his eye. Sayuwoe waved at him until she got his attention, and then motioned him to come to her kitchen.

"Quick! Get me some water and a washcloth...and some soap," she said to Myatu.

Myatu got up, as fast as she could hurry her steps, and rushed to the water barrel sitting beside the family hut. The children quickly turned their assaults at her, mocking the way she jerked her legs to move fast. Myatu hastily dipped cups of water out of the barrel and into the basin. She hurried back to the kitchen, reaching Sayuwoe the same time the old man reached their kitchen. To lighten the girl's load, Sayuwoe collected the basin, put it on the table and offered the old man the stool she had been sitting on.

"I have never seen you before," Sayuwoe said to him. "Are you from around here?"

"I'm not from here," the old man answered, slightly out of breath. "I come from Siah (see-i) Village."

"Siah Village is two days' walk from here," Sayuwoe said to Myatu, suggesting the old man had come from afar. Then she asked the old man, "Is it not so?"

"Yes," the old man confirmed.

"Have you come to visit a relative?" Sayuwoe asked, as if getting information to help him find his relatives, had he been visiting.

"I do not know anyone in this village," the old man replied. "I reached your village at sundown and decided to rest here before continuing to Siah Village."

"Rest here in Monomono Village?" Sayuwoe questioned with a chuckle, but with no intent of being impolite. She knew that people in Monomono Village did not care for poor newcomers. "If you only knew, you would not have stopped here," she said to him. "People here are not pleasant to strangers who appear poor. The way you're dressed, and I am not looking down on you, my friend, these people are certain to treat you unfavorably. That is the reason for the children's ugly habits. [4]Good-friend...let me take care of your wound."

The old man sat down and Sayuwoe got to work. She soaked the towel and began to gently sponge down the bruise.

"Why are these children cruel to an old man?" he asked.

"Can an orange fall far from its tree?" Sayuwoe replied with a parable. "The children are like their parents. They would be spiteful even to an old woman. People here are swollen with pride...it is be-

---

4 *To address a stranger in a friendly manner*

cause they own more wealth than most."

Sayuwoe went on with more details about the villagers' unduly high opinions of themselves, to which the old man responded 'uh' and 'aw', but his attention had long since shifted to the pot of leftovers. She took note of it and asked Myatu to prepare some food for their guest.

Myatu's face did not show the slightest sign of displeasure because of the task placed on her. She got up, fetched a clean bowl, and dished out some food from the leftovers pot. She made sure the food looked neat, without any dripping on the brim, and placed it on the table with a spoon; all the while smiling.

"What happened to your daughter?" the old man asked Sayuwoe, when he noticed Myatu wobbling back to her stool.

Sayuwoe gave him a doubtful, but friendly, stare and then broke out into uncontrollable laughter. He chuckled as well, not knowing the reason for her laughter.

"Since when can an old woman have a young daughter?" Sayuwoe said to him. "Myatu is my granddaughter. Her mother died during childbirth and I have cared for her since. Myatu was born a cripple."

Sayuwoe neglected explaining every detail of Myatu's disability. She finished tending the old man's wound and cleared the table to make space for the food Myatu had prepared. The old man grabbed his spoon and gobbled down all the food Myatu set before him.

"You should spend the night here with us," Sayuwoe offered. "It is too late to walk the rest of the way, especially traveling alone."

"I will be fine," the old man said. "In fact, I will be leaving you shortly because I do not want my family to get worried. I have taken up too much of your time already and I do not want to trouble you any further."

He got up to prepare to leave.

"It is no trouble at all," Sayuwoe insisted. "Leave tomorrow morning...as early as you'd like. Myatu and I get up early on Wednesdays so we get to the market on time. We'll make sure that you are up and ready to leave before dawn."

"No need to worry, I'll be fine," he said. "I only wish that I had something to give you. The money that I had in my pocket might have dropped while running away from the children."

Sayuwoe smiled at the implication. He looked as if he had nothing to begin with, she thought. It did not matter; she had done it out of the goodness of her heart.

"Why did you tell me that people in your village are not kind to poor people?" he said to Sayuwoe.

"Because, they are not," Sayuwoe replied.

"You and your granddaughter have redeemed your people," the old man said. "I am witness to it...there are some good people in Monomono Village."

"Everyone is not bad, mind you," Sayuwoe said quickly, "but, the awful ones outnumber those that are good. Many years ago when I moved here from Gwapala, the people in Monomono Village welcomed me. It was because of my business...I am a basket weaver. Life here was not bad for me, only losing my daughter has been heartbreaking. My daughter, Liopu, was married to one of their prominent countrymen, a man called Gbarzon, Myatu's father. At one time, Gbarzon was a...."

While Sayuwoe was still talking, the old man got up and walked quietly to the stack of unfinished baskets. He bent toward the heap of baskets to take a closer look. Sayuwoe joined him and then Myatu followed.

He laid his hand against the basket, sitting at the top, and began rubbing his fingers against it, like a blind person would. "Even the unfinished ones are beautiful," he said. "I like the different patterns that you used on this one. The rods are plated in more directions than I have ever seen. It is beautiful...this is beautiful."

"Myatu made that one...and it is not yet finished," Sayuwoe bragged. "She gets better at it every day. Every month people come to the market in great numbers to see her new designs."

"She is a special girl," the old man said, smiling.

"Yes, my Myatu is special," Sayuwoe agreed and then asked, "Have you been to Botota Market?"

"I have not," the old man replied.

Sayuwoe gave him a puzzling stare. "You should go there and see for yourself," she said. "There is no place like it in the world. The sight is even wonderful!"

"Wonderful?" the old man said, jokingly.

"Wonderful," Sayuwoe repeated. "I am sure that people from your village go there to buy their goods. Everybody goes to Botota Market. Before I moved to Monomono Village, I had only heard about it. I could not believe my eyes when I first visited the place."

"I hope to see this place someday," the old man said.

"Let that day be on the second Wednesday of the month," Sayuwoe suggested. "Myatu and I are there selling our baskets. Come and find us when you come to the market."

"I will," he promised.

Sayuwoe thought of those things that were at hand and necessary for the old man's journey. She went to her fruit basket and collected two mangos, one banana, and three oranges, and dropped them in a small hand-netted bag. "This is for your journey," she said and handed him the bag.

He collected the bag from Sayuwoe, but kept his eyes on Myatu. "Please, tell me your name again," he said to Myatu. "Old men have short memories."

Myatu said her name shyly, "Myatu."

"Myatu, you are as beautiful as the moonlight," the old man said. "I'm sure you've been told this before."

Myatu smiled. "I have never been told that," she said, shaking her head.

"You are as beautiful as a full moon...and I can assure you, your wishes will come true one day."

Myatu shrugged her shoulders and smiled.

"It will," the old man repeated.

"Will I see my father again?" Myatu asked, partly for the sake of conversation.

"I do not know...and that is not the wish I'm talking about. Is there not something you've wished for, other than seeing your father? Search your heart, my dear daughter, because it is there."

"I have no other wish," Myatu said. "I only wish to see my father."

"Search your heart," the old man said and started to walk away.

"You have not told us your name," Sayuwoe's inquiry stopped him.

"My name is, Ayordajee (*i-yor-doe-ge*)," he replied.

Sayuwoe repeated his name in her mind. She had had many customers over the years, but his name was not familiar. "Go well, good friend," she said, "let God go with you."

"Look at the full moon," Ayordajee pointed toward the sky.

Sayuwoe and Myatu looked up. There was a bright band of stars stretching from horizon to horizon and the moon seemed more silvery than blue.

"A silvery moon means one thing," Ayordajee said.

"What does it mean?" Sayuwoe asked.

"The night is a good night," he said. "I will be safe. The old people from my village say that a full moon is like a pie. The moonlight is a little touch of heaven on earth…a piece of pie for each person to enjoy."

Sayuwoe thought otherwise. Tekoa and Liopu died on full moon nights. Gbarzon staged his abandonment on a full moon night. As far as she was concern, she did not care to see another full moon night.

"What is there to enjoy on a full moon night?" Sayuwoe asked.

Ayordajee looked at Myatu. "What the moon leaves behind," he said and quietly walked away.

The women watched him stroll away with unhurrying feet. Then his body dimmed and disappeared into the night.

"Did you notice his hand?" Sayuwoe asked.

"No, grandmother, I did not...why?"

"There is something different about him," Sayuwoe muttered. "I cannot pinpoint it, but his hands do not belong to a poor man. How could a poor man know so much about expensive designs?"

"Why then is he dressed like one?" Myatu asked. "Monomono Village is no place to pretend as if you're poor. Perhaps he did not know this."

"Myatu, you should have noticed his hands."

"I would not have seen them in the dark," Myatu insisted.

"You are not observant about things," Sayuwoe said. "You ought to be more observant, my child. Use *all* the senses God has given to you. I saw his hands clearly in the moonlight."

Myatu looked at her grandmother and held her peace, refusing to deal with Sayuwoe's pressing way of persuasion. "Tomorrow we have to take the baskets to the market…let's go to bed early, I am tired," she cleverly changed topic.

Then Myatu took the cup the old man had used, filled it with water, and sprinkled water on the half-dead coals. She waited until she saw fluttering ashes in the gray smoke, confirming the fire had died, and prepared to leave.

"Good-night, Grandmother," she muttered and left Sayuwoe to go in the hut.

"Good night, Myatu," Sayuwoe replied.

Sayuwoe did a quick visual inspection of the kitchen, making sure it was clean from top to bottom. Then she found the lantern, filled it with kerosene, lit the wick and followed Myatu into the hut.

Night passed peacefully in the village.

As for Sayuwoe, much was not remembered between midnight and dawn. Then, from the outskirts of the village, the cries of the pepper birds declared dawn.

Sayuwoe opened her eyes and peeped at the plank bedroom window. From the small opening where the wood barely came together, outside looked dim. She reluctantly pulled off her favorite hand-loomed blanket; the one Liopu made her, and prepared to get up.

Still under the influence of sleep, Sayuwoe got up and sat at the edge of her straw-stuffed bed. "My bed needs more straw...I can feel the hard frame," she complained, while pounding the mattress with her hand.

Surprisingly, Myatu did not wake to the annoying hand beats. Except for the breathing movement of her body, moving up and down, one would think she was dead. Sayuwoe got up and tiptoed over to Myatu's bed, a space of three feet, to see if she was sleeping. Her eyes were shut, but with the closing one could easily tell it was a fake closing.

"Myatu, wake up," Sayuwoe said. She lay her hand on Myatu's hip and gently shook her. "Myatu...Myatu?"

Myatu's face broke into a smile, to which Sayuwoe found bothersome; the girl was not sleeping, just lying there.

"We have to go to the market early, remember?" Sayuwoe said.

Myatu fully stretched her arms and legs to release her limbs from the long night, her eyes still closed. Then, she pulled the covers back up to her shoulders. "Grandmother, I was having a beautiful dream," she said, in a sleep-headed voice.

"Do you know what today is? Get up," Sayuwoe repeated.

Myatu threw her covers off and slowly got up, at a snail's pace. She sat at the edge of her bed.

"You move as if you have no plans for the day," Sayuwoe said.

"Are you not feeling well?" She touched Myatu's forehead to check for fever. She felt warm, but not feverish. "If you are sick, we can stay home today."

"I am not sick, Grandmother," Myatu said.

"Get ready so we can go to the market," Sayuwoe said and walked away.

Myatu remain sitting.

"Are you going with me to the market today?"

"Yes, Grandmother, I am going with you," Myatu said and then asked, "Do you remember what the old man told me last night?"

Sayuwoe thought for a brief moment. "I do not remember," she said.

"He asked if I had any wishes."

"Now, I remember," Sayuwoe said. "Did Gbarzon come home last night?"

"No," Myatu shook her head.

"Do you have another wish?"

"Yes," Myatu said, hesitantly.

Sayuwoe looked around the room. "Where is it," she asked. "I do not see anything that is new in here."

"You cannot see it, Grandmother…it was in my dream."

Sayuwoe fought hard to hide her anger, mainly because she did not care to discuss Gbarzon's leaving nor his whereabouts. She left Myatu sitting on her bed and strolled back to her own bed. Sayuwoe reached underneath it and pulled out the basket of neatly folded lappas. Usually her daily outfit is carefully chosen, but without giving much thought, Sayuwoe grabbed the first lappa she touched, tucked it under her arm, and headed for the washroom. She noticed Myatu still sitting on her bed and stopped.

"Myatu, I want us to get to the market on time," Sayuwoe said, as if pleading.

Myatu remained sitting.

Sayuwoe abandoned her trip to the washroom, threw the lappa on the bed, and walked back to Myatu's bed. "Did you see Gbarzon in your dream last night?" she said, slightly irritated.

"No," Myatu muttered.

"Okay, Myatu, please…tell me about your wish."

Myatu smiled.

"Go on," Sayuwoe said, also smiling.

"Oh, Grandmother, I've never experienced anything like it," Myatu said. "It seemed so real."

"Tell me," Sayuwoe said.

"In my dream last night, I was the most beautiful girl in our village," Myatu said, excitedly.

Sayuwoe smiled and waited to hear more. She knew all about Myatu's misery; the soreness and loneliness like the horror of being a [5]bat. While growing up, those in Myatu's age group flatly refused her friendship so she had never occupied herself with anyone other than Sayuwoe.

"Myatu, have I not told you, you are the most beautiful girl in Monomono Village," Sayuwoe said. "You do not need to be told in a dream."

"I know what you've said to me, Grandmother, but my legs remind me. I am not beautiful...no one has come to offer a dowry for me. I am twenty-one years old, a grown woman, yet it is my grandmother who shares her home with me, not my husband. My mother got married much younger than my age, is it not so?"

"Yes," Sayuwoe nodded.

"Did she not dance in front of Gbarzon, to the point that he cried? You told me their story."

"That is true," Sayuwoe said and added, "Gbarzon was so happy to have a beautiful wife, he danced himself beyond exhaustion."

"See Grandmother...it is different for me," Myatu said. "I am not a beautiful girl, like my mother. Instead, I am a crippled bat and people do not wait to go behind my back to laugh at me. They do it to my face," Myatu cried.

"Myatu, my child, the good thing that God has for you is sure to come. One day the man who sees your beauty in his heart will come to claim you. He will see your beauty with his eyes, not the eyes of these people in Monomono Village."

"Nobody is coming, Grandmother, nobody is coming here to claim me," Myatu sobbed. "Have you heard of any man who wants

5 *According to an African tale, Bat was lonely and his loneliness began eating him up on the inside, so he decided to visit with the birds to see whether they would welcome him. When the birds noted the absence of a beak and other un-birdlike characteristics of bat, they sent him off to the other animals. When he got there, the animals saw only the ways he was more like a bird. They, too, would not have him either. It was one thing or another. Belonging nowhere, Bat continued to ache for people of his own. One hears this ache in his crying during the night.*

a wife that cannot dance at her own wedding? Dancing is in our blood…a bride must be able to dance before her husband."

"Not every bride is expected to dance," Sayuwoe argued.

"Every bride, Grandmother, every bride," Myatu insisted.

"Is it your wish?" Sayuwoe asked. "Do you want to be a dancer or a bride?"

"A dancer," Myatu said and stood up. "I wish to be the best dancer…like I was in my dream."

"Tell me," Sayuwoe said.

"Dancers from Monomono Village were joined with other dancers from faraway villages to compete for the Africa's Finest Dancer title," Myatu started. "The drummers pounded different drums with strong beats…the women rattled their [6]*sasas*…yes, Grandmother, the harmony of tune and rhythm filled the air. All the dancers, dressed in fine clothes, leaped and skipped about excitedly. While they were dancing, I stood by the side, alone, watching. The music was wonderful, so I tried to move my legs, but I could not. No matter how hard I tried, I could not move.

"Then a strange thing happened…the rhythm reached my heart and the beats lured me into the tune. Little by little, my toes began moving…then my feet…and then my legs. Soon my entire body was moving and I started dancing. It was as if my legs were normal. I danced and danced. I even danced better than all the other girls did. Guess what, Grandmother?"

"What?"

"I, Myatu, was declared the winner!"

"You were?"

"Yes…and while the chief was placing the winner's wreath around my neck, the heavy drumbeats subsided to soft thumping. I woke up and saw you hitting your mattress," Myatu said, laughing.

"I am sorry to have ruined your dream," Sayuwoe said, also laughing.

"How could you have known, Grandmother? It was a dream."

"Myatu, in the real world, you are the most beautiful girl in Monomono Village. In fact, you are the most beautiful girl in the whole world," Sayuwoe said and drew Myatu between her shoulders.

---

6 *Instruments made by threading beads, seeds, or shells on stings, which cradled the whole calabash. As the strings are jerked, the seeds snap against the gourds, making a cha-cha sound*

At that moment, a sudden hard constant knock on the front door caught them by surprise, followed by a man's soft calling, "Sayuwoe! Sayuwoe!"

Sayuwoe left Myatu standing and rushed to the door.

"Who is it?" she asked, without opening the door.

"Zahawe," the man replied.

Sayuwoe did not recognize the name, but opened the door with just enough space to see her caller without him seeing her. The morning had barely grown enough light to see much, still Sayuwoe could tell from his appearance he was an important man. Other than the chief, it was impossible for a local of any village to receive a royal personality. Even her famous customers were preceded by their servants. Either the man had selected the wrong hut, or he had come himself to buy a basket. Nevertheless, her customers knew to find her at the market on the second Wednesday of every month.

"Are you Sayuwoe?" the man asked, spying at the small space between the door and doorframe.

Sayuwoe opened the door and stepped outside. The man looked bold and handsome, as if he had been sharply carved out of some splendid brown wood.

"I am Sayuwoe," she replied, a little shaky but not much for him to notice.

"I am Zahawe, Prince of Siah Village," he said, politely extending his hand.

Sayuwoe did not concur, seemingly caught by surprise. She stood staring at his innocent doe-eyes and spruce looks. Prince Zahawe was wearing an ornament made of platinum gold around his neck, studded with diamonds. On his arms were several gold bracelets that went from his wrist up to his elbow. His black sleeveless outer garment, opened down the front, was embroidered with gold threads of hibiscus patterns. And a heavy ribbed silk belt, with floral motifs in gold thread, held up his long pants. The engraved centerpiece on his belt was made of pure gold, decorated with eleven rubies, featuring a lion's head made of ivory.

Surely, he had not come to buy baskets, Sayuwoe thought, seeing the crew of about fifty servants and twenty-five decorated diplomats accompanying him.

"Please, forgive me," Prince Zahawe apologized and lowered his hand. "I am sorry if I have disturbed or frightened you. It is Myatu that I have come to see. I was told I would find her here. Does she not live here?"

"My granddaughter," Sayuwoe stuttered. "Yes...she lives here."

Myatu managed to reach the door, just as Sayuwoe spoke her name. She wobbled out and stood by Sayuwoe.

"Are you Myatu," Zahawe asked.

Myatu nodded.

Zahawe looked at her and stepped back.

"Father was right," he whispered. "You are as beautiful as a full moon...exceptionally pleasing in one's eyes."

Myatu looked at Sayuwoe, a puzzling stare.

"Who are you, really?" Sayuwoe asked. "Why have you come here?"

"I am Zahawe, prince of Siah Village. I have come to seek my bride." Then he turned toward the entourage of men accompanying him. "Tell her father...tell them that I have come in goodwill."

Ayordajee swiftly emerged out of the crowd, wearing a handsome three-piece outfit. His outfit was made of hand-loomed material with elegant matching embroidery gold designs. The [7]*buba*, pants, and hat were one-of-a-kind, unique and sophisticated. The entire outfit was covered with brown, white, and gold crown-triangle design patterns.

"Ayordajee?" Sayuwoe said, hardly recognizing the old man, had it not been the bruise above his eye.

"Yes, Sayuwoe, it is me...."

"The old man from last night," Sayuwoe cried.

"Yes, Sayuwoe...I am the old man from last night. Prince Zahawe is my son and he has come to claim a bride," Ayordajee confirmed. "Sayuwoe, should you agree, I will give you enough *dowry* for your beautiful granddaughter. Would you consider our offer?"

Sayuwoe stood in tearful silence. "What are you saying," she mumbled, finally.

"Would you accept our offer," Ayordajee pleaded.

"What offer?" Sayuwoe asked, astonished. "No amount of money can be considered for the troubles the moon has left behind for my granddaughter. Even silver dishes and golden spoons could never give her satisfaction. For Myatu, I want a husband who will love her,

---

7 *Fashionable men's robe or dressing gown*

live with her honestly and treat her decently. And in the course of time, let God bless them with children so those children can come to my hut, from time to time, to hear stories about Liopu and Tekoa."

"Then, Zahawe will be that man," Ayordajee said. "Zahawe listens to the needs of our people; he will listen to the needs of his wife. My son will lay down his life for his wife."

"I must be dreaming," Myatu murmured.

"You are not dreaming Myatu," Ayordajee said to her. "The moon has left behind a prince, begging for your heart. We traveled all night on the shoulders of our servants to reach before dawn. Neither Zahawe nor I was bothered by the rough hammock ride. I wanted us at your door by dawn. Myatu, answer me this once, have you not wished for a husband?"

Myatu smiled. "Yes," she murmured.

By now, the morning sun had risen over Monomono Village with dazzling beauty. Dew soaked heavy on everything and each droplet of water refraction intensified the brilliance of the sun. Many of the villagers, heading to Botota Market, saw the crowd in Sayuwoe's yard and stopped to inquire news of her elegant company. In a little while, a thick gathering of inquisitive spectators crowded the front yard.

Myatu saw the crowd and her eyes welled with tears. Her light brown eyes were glittering, telling all that her heart was feeling. She held her face high to keep the tears from falling, but it was no use. Tears came streaming down her checks.

Prince Zahawe walked to Myatu and stood before her. Then, using his thumb, he gently wiped each drop of tear that fell on Myatu's face, showing a simple gesture of compassion and concern for his bride-to-be. "Myatu, will you marry me," Prince Zahawe asked. "Say 'yes' so I can beg for your grandmother's blessings because she holds the key to your heart."

Myatu looked at Sayuwoe, Sayuwoe nodded.

"Yes, Prince Zahawe," Myatu said, "I would be honored to be your bride."

Prince Zahawe pulled Myatu between his shoulders and gently wrapped his arms around her. The musicians, standing at the back of the entourage, began blowing their pipes, strumming their harps, and pounding their drums. Their music shook the earth on which Monomono Village sat. Even people living deep in the village heard it while they began planning their workday and asked the reason for the noise, since the village did not seem to be in uproar. Later, those who stopped by Sayuwoe's yard took them the news; a prince from Siah Village had come to Monomono Village to engage one of their own, the cripple girl. Many could not believe an important prince had come to get himself a wife wrapped in such an ordinary package.

As the music touched his heart, Prince Zahawe lifted Myatu in his arms. She wrapped her arms around his neck, rested her head on his shoulder, and closed her eyes. He began dancing, moving his body and feet in rhythm, lightly and merrily.

"You have chosen a girl who has no royal blood," Sayuwoe said to Ayordajee. "You could have chosen the daughter of another chief, someone with royal blood, to match your son's blood."

"Why do we look at people for their outward appearance, when we should be looking at their heart," Ayordajee replied. "Because of it, we miss the wonderful things people are made of."

"You are right," Sayuwoe said. Then she called, "Myatu! Myatu! Not only are you the most beautiful woman in Monomono Village, you are the best dancer. Look at them...they're all watching you," she pointed.

Myatu opened her eyes and saw the crowd.

SONGS OF THE PEPPER BIRDS

Oldman Jallah (*jah-la*) had many stories for which there were many listening ears. Receiving company from dawn until dusk, the small kitchen next to his tidy one-room hut stayed occupied with influential chiefs and important nobles from faraway places, many seeking his counsel. Those living in Twoku (*tu-ku*) Village came to see him as well. Some brought with them food, money, clothing or items of household use. Of all the things that Oldman Jallah received, he was generous in giving all away to those who needed them. He made use of his gifts for other people's needs and kept only the few things he used.

One late afternoon while roasting a [1]cassava in the glowing embers of his hearth, Kaimu (*ca-moon*), a local palm-wine tapper showed up. Oldman Jallah was not expecting any guests, except for the children who come after dinner to huddle around his fire to hear folktales.

"Hello, Oldman Jallah," Kaimu greeted in a sad voice.

Oldman Jallah did not raise his head, occupied with tending his cassava, but he instinctively took hold of Kaimu's extended hand. The two men shook hands, [2]snapping their middle fingers.

"I'm sorry for coming late," Kaimu apologized before Oldman Jallah could ask his guest of his welfare. "I see that you have not had your dinner."

Oldman Jallah glanced at Kaimu, whose face looked troubling. "It is okay, Kaimu, I am happy to receive even unexpected guests," he said. Then he flipped the cassava over to keep it from burning and added, "It seems as if joy has gone out of you. What's wrong?"

Kaimu made no answer and continue standing.

---

1 (Yucca) a bulky starchy root (tuber) about 1 mm thick, rough, and brown on the outside, the flesh of the root is chalk-white color.
2 Liberians end a handshake by snapping their middle fingers, which parts with a popping noise.

"Sit down," Oldman Jallah said, pointing at the old stool standing in the corner. "When a man's heart is sore, it is always because of a woman or his money. Which is it?"

Kaimu heaved a sigh, took the stool, placed it next to the mat, and sat mute.

"In life there is no down without an up," Oldman Jallah said, looking at Kaimu. "What is troubling you?"

Kaimu thought it wise to hurriedly voice his concerns to give the old man chance to eat his dinner. He also wanted to buy time in finding the right place to start in his tale.

"Do you know Nyawa (*na-whe*)?" Kiamu asked.

"Isn't she Josef Yeke's (*yek-kei*) daughter?"

"Yes," Kaimu nodded.

"Ah...Kaimu, are you putting your walking stick where your hand cannot reach?" Oldman Jallah joked, knowing the young woman belonged to a family of some rank.

"Perhaps," Kaimu replied and then said underneath his breath, "Nyawa and I slept together one night last week."

"You two are not married," Oldman Jallah cried. "Are you prepared to marry Josef Yeke's daughter?"

Kaimu sensed doubt in Oldman Jallah's voice and made no answer.

"Kaimu, you have fed this hunger in your heart like any other man," Oldman Jallah cautioned. "Have you created a problem in hope of turning it to an opportunity?"

"No," Kaimu said quickly.

"Are you going to marry Josef Yeke's daughter?" Oldman Jallah asked, putting emphasis on the 'Josef Yeke' name.

"I do not have that kind of money," Kaimu muttered.

Oldman Jallah cleverly read between the lines. Seemingly, Kaimu had made for himself a bed shorter than he could stretch himself on, with coverings narrower than he can wrap himself in. The old man remembered his dinner and juggled the charred cassava out of the fire with his bare hands. Obviously parched, he dropped it to the side and poked the scorched skin with the knife; it was still edible.

"This is a big problem," Oldman Jallah said, nodding his head. "It may even be impossible. However, all impossibilities compel us to rely on God. I know that you have come for my advice. What can I say? First, tell me. Do you love this woman?"

Kaimu looked at the old man, but he could not spill a word out of his mouth. The mental weight of the predicament seemed to have suspended his voice.

"Well, I see you have not come for my advice," Oldman Jallah said. "You ought to be talking to Josef Yeke, not me. Go and tell Nyawa's father what you have just told me."

"What do you mean?" Kaimu asked.

Oldman Jallah gave Kaimu a pathetic stare, for the cowardliness of his false claim, pretending not to understand what he was implying.

"I...I cannot do it," Kaimu stuttered. "If I do, he will bring charges against me. What am I to do then? I do not have that kind of money to pay him."

"Even if you do not have the *dowry* now, maybe some arrangements can be made. Josef Yeke is a reasonable man, I know him well."

"That is not the issue," Kaimu said.

"What is the issue?"

Kaimu could not tell the issue.

"Kaimu, if this thing is too hard for you, go home and come back tomorrow," Oldman Jallah advised and picked up the roasted cassava, which by now had reached tolerable warmth.

He held one end of the cassava and scraped the surface as hard as his frail arm allowed him. Then he diced it into small pieces and put the pieces in the bowl. Still waiting for Kaimu's decision, Oldman Jallah poured [3]*palm oil* sparingly over the cassava pieces and sprinkled some salt for seasoning. All this time, Kaimu rested his shaky hands on his lap and remained mute.

"Let me ask you something," Oldman Jallah said, looking directly at Kaimu. "Are you troubled by the disgrace you have brought to this woman's character? Or, is it the money you will be asked to pay?"

Kaimu remained mute.

"Why are your hands trembling?" Oldman Jallah asked. "Either way, she must become your wife. What man would want a woman who has already been [4]spoiled by another man? When you are married, who is to know your business?"

"I never wanted to disgrace Nyawa," Kaimu mumbled. "It was

3 *Red oil produced by skimming the pounded pulp of the palm nut.*
4 *No longer a virgin*

never my plan."

"Whether it's a plan or an intention, there's always *intent* when people get together. It is later, much later, and then the man is not capable of doing what comes next, which is honoring the woman. It is hard to tell who is courting whom in this village...unless a *dowry* is paid. Anyway, have you been courting Nyawa behind her father's back? How else would you have gone to see her?"

"She came to see me," Kaimu corrected.

"Of course," Oldman Jallah said, aware of Josef Yeke's overly protectiveness for his family, especially his three daughters.

"But that is not the problem," Kaimu said.

"Um...get to the problem then."

"We have been courting in secret," Kaimu said, "And it is only because I do not have enough money to pay a full dowry. Nyawa knows I love her very much."

"In that case, why have you not gone to her people? You have come to me instead...speak truthfully my son, why does this love frighten you? Love is the only power capable of conquering a man's heart. But love is not *love* until you give it away openly."

Kaimu stood up and shoved the stool, out of frustration. Then he covered his heart with both hands and looked toward the ceiling, as if petitioning. "If you only knew," he mumbled and dropped his hands.

"Your answer is not in my ceiling," Oldman Jallah scolded. "You ought to search your heart. Have you told me everything? How am I to help you if you are withholding your thoughts? Your face tells me there is more, but I cannot read your mind."

"Nyawa's dowry has already been paid," Kaimu cried.

"Then, there is no problem. If you have already paid the dowry, what more would her father want?"

Kaimu mumbled, "By another man," and took in a long breath.

Oldman Jallah took a piece of cassava between his dusty charred fingers, mashed it, and stuffed his mouth. He finished working his chew, grabbed the cup of water sitting next to his mat, sipped it, and put down the cup.

Kaimu exhaled and waited.

"What you have done is the cruelest crime against another man," Oldman Jallah rebuked angrily. "How could you? What has made you do such wickedness? You are going to pay dearly for it," he pointed at Kaimu.

"I do not have any money! How am I to pay what I do not have?" Kaimu said, pulling out the pockets from the sides of his trousers.

"What has that got to do with it? Who will pay for this? You," Oldman Jallah shouted. "No matter how long it takes, truth buried in the past comes out. Sooner or later this will be known. You must go and face her people. You have willingly brought shame on you, so it is left with you to become honorable again. Listen to me, Kaimu."

"I am listening, Oldman Jallah, I'm listening," Kaimu said. "I hear what you're telling me."

"A man must give account of his deeds, no matter how painful," Oldman Jallah went on. "When God has His hand on your troubles, it becomes a small thing compare with the judgment of a [5]big man. Although Josef Yeke dips his hands in the [6]kola nut bowl to fulfill justice among the people of Twoku Village, God fulfills justice to all, including those beyond our boundaries. Mind my words, your spirit will remain down until you do the right thing."

Kaimu hung his head, humbled by Oldman Jallah's harsh reproof. He had expected a firm, but modest counsel. Nevertheless, the old man's criticism was small compared to the trail in front of Josef Yeke, a lawgiver in Twoku Village.

"Memories trouble old men," Oldman Jallah continued. "It is not 'they say', I know it. Do not allow this crime to be planted negatively in your memory. If Josef Yeke is puffed up, to the point where he becomes unreasonable, you must bear it and do so, humbly. After all, two cannot quarrel when one will not. You are the one who have wronged him by stealing his daughter's pride. Let me share a story with you before the children arrive."

Kaimu lifted his head, reposition the stool, and sat straighter.

"Many years ago in Suacoco, my hometown, there was none to be so much praised as Ayima (*i-ye-ma*), who was beautiful and pleasant to look at. From the crown of her head to the sole of her feet, no blemish was found on her. Every man that saw Ayima, wanted to claim her. However, the dowry for the daughter of a prosperous chief is costly. Not many men can afford it. But money does not measure love for everyone. Ayima fell in love with a man with neither wealth

---

5 *One with power or authority*
6 *Kola nut symbolizes peace offering, offered to visitors or used by a council of elders, when palava (argument or difference of opinion) is judged*

nor status, and they were forced to court in secret.

"When Ayima's dowry negotiation was at hand, the richest man in the entire region came to her father to offer payment. Palakwolli (*pa-la-quel-le*) was a great man among his people. He owned more than seven thousand sheep and goats; three thousand cows and he had an innumerable amount of land. Every one of his forty wives wore imported garments, when other women only heard of them. Each wife took turns having feasts, serving only imported rum and well-refined wines.

Regardless of all that Palakwolli was blessed with, he was mean-spirited. Dressed with great authority, from his shoulders and upward, his body stood higher than any man among his people. Men flinched on his command. Palakwolli would say to a man, 'go', and he would go; and to another, 'come', and he would come, and to others, 'do this', and they would do it. His followers were fruitful in their duties only because they feared him, heeding to his demands no matter how degrading. Those who did not fear Palakwolli were told they had no appreciation for life.

"In spite of his vicious personality, Chief Balomah accepted Palakwolli's offer. Ayima pleaded with her father that she did not want the marriage, but Chief Balomah went ahead and set a date for the wedding anyhow and invited important guests.

"Ayima pressed her lover hard, even beyond reasoning, that he arrange a runaway journey for them. He declined her request at first, knowing the risk could cost him his life. However, Ayima pushed harder until he planned their escape.

"Of course, the absence of the chief's daughter became noticeable right away. Chief Balomah accused Palakwolli of claiming his bride disrespectfully; Palakwolli accused Chief Balomah of hiding his daughter. Accusations were tossed from side to side, until Palakwolli got tired of it. To prove his sincerity, he hired one hundred warriors to search for Ayima. Palakwolli ordered the men to find her with the threat that if they did not return his bride, he would separate their heads from their shoulders.

"The men searched the region far and wide. At some time during the search, when the men did not know of Ayima's whereabouts, Palakwolli even beheaded a man and no one had the boldness to question him.

"The couple continued their escape deep into the forest. After traveling inside the jungle for seven days, eating only wild berries, fruits, and nuts, they reached the Cavalla River. But there were no means of crossing the giant river that was surrounded by thick bushes. Ayima felt reasonably safe although the surroundings were inhabited with untamed creatures and giant reptiles. Her lover had made sure of it, always walking a step ahead of her to shield her from danger. The couple waited with hope that perhaps someone would come to the river and take them across it. Even after waiting two days, no one had shown up.

"After collecting dry twigs and branches, with Ayima's help, he built a fire for the night. The crackling fire kept them safe. The night was peaceful, except for the shrill sounds of night birds, insects, and bullfrogs. During the night, Ayima looked forward for the first light when the pepper birds made their early morning cries. She loved the songs of the pepper birds, a fast-becoming sacred song for her freedom.

"As time passed, the chance of escaping from Palakwolli seemed useless. Closely trailing them were Palakwolli and his men. Then it happened. Without warning, a cleverly planned two-sided raid trapped the couple. The men carefully laid hands on Ayima's shoulder, but roughly arrested her companion. Ayima did not want to return. She kicked and slapped at the men until she broke away, and then she jumped into the river. She came to the surface just once and then sank to rise no more. Palakwolli demanded that they pluck out her body, but leave behind the eight men who drowned trying to save her. Their bodies were to remain in the water until the river decided to give up her dead.

"Ayima's friend was bounded and they dragged him back to the village, leaving behind a trail of his blood. He stood before Chief Balomah at the judgment hall and it was determined that because Palakwolli would have become Ayima's husband, it was Palakwolli who was to decide the punishment. Twenty-five years of backbreaking labor was Palakwolli's judgment. The man was to pay back the bride price that Chief Balomah had received, plus the cost for his arrest. Palakwolli made his life miserable with hard bondage in all manner of service. He cleared an entire forest for Palakwolli's farming and planted rice and cassava. He waited on Palakwolli's wives in running their errands. When Palakwolli could no longer get any use out of him, he set the man free.

"As for Chief Balomah, he mourned his daughter's passing for three months, refusing food and drinks. He received no visitors until after two years. The beautiful Ayima became a memory rather than becoming my wife," Oldman Jallah's voice choked.

Kaimu lifted his head and looked at the old man, caught by surprise. "Oldman Jallah, I'm sorry," he muttered.

"You see, Kaimu, I failed her," Oldman Jallah said. "It was my place to show Ayima the proper thing to do. Instead, I caused her to lose her life. Those that judged me, rightfully accused me when they called me a princess killer. I should have talked to her father, although I did not have the money or land. Perhaps Ayima would have been alive today…sharing my life in my old age…I was selfish. Over the years, I've prayed every night to see her in my dreams. The only comfort that life gives me is the pepper birds. I wake up at the crack of dawn to hear the cries of the pepper birds. During our travel in the jungle, Ayima prevented me from talking so she could hear their cries."

Kaimu noticed the clumped oil-soaked cassava pieces in the bowl and thought the old man's supper had sat untouched for too long. He got up and tried to leave.

"Kaimu, do not betray your heart," Oldman Jallah said. "Who knows? Even to gray hair, this love will carry you. Let yours end differently. Do you love her?"

"Yes," Kaimu said, "I love her very much."

"Then remember, your character is only as strong as your deeds. Go to Josef Yeke and talk with him so you reclaim your honor."

Kaimu nodded. He started to leave, but was stopped to the old man's calling.

"Kaimu…I will go with you to Josef Yeke and speak on your behalf…only if you need me to."

"I need you to," Kaimu begged, and then he walked away, pacing his steps slowly back to his home.

Oldman Jallah waited until Kaimu disappeared into dark distant, then he took the bowl of cassava, set it on his lap, and hand-fed his mouth until every scrap of cassava was consumed.

As he finished drinking his water, the children arrived. They settled gleefully, habitually cramming the space in the front. Either their little faces were propped in both palms or their chins were held high.

"Once upon a time," Oldman Jallah called for their attention.

"Time!" the group of children responded. Everyone sat forward-bent and their little eager eyes were staring directly at Oldman Jallah's mouth.

"There once lived a man named Oluma, and he was the richest man in Gbataalah. Oluma credited his wealth to a [7]*Mammy-Water,* believed to be living in a special creek near the village. Oluma advised those who envied him to take care, because they could be cursed like his best friend, Momolu, who was found near the creek with his belly opened early one morning. He accused Phephena, *(fe-fe-na)* an old medicine woman living in the forest, of putting a spell on Momolu while they were hunting [8]*fullingtonga* one night. Oluma was spared from Phephena's spell because he jumped into the creek and had remained hiding underneath the water. He claimed it was the mermaid's good fortune that saved him and thereafter, blessed him with all his fortune.

"Phephena was her given name but because she spent so much time in the jungle collecting leaves for her *juju,* the people called her Mama Lion. It was believed that Mama Lion's special powers allowed her to throw lightning when she wanted to, even during the daytime while the sun was hottest. She also mysteriously compelled criminals to confess, and at times, placed on them deserving punishments.

"Many witnessed how her spell exposed a thief. Once when a goat was stolen in the village, the owner went to see her. Mama Lion placed some leaves in a white cloth, tied a bright red string around it, and told the man to place the *juju* over the gate to his establishment. He was to warn the people in the village that within two days or less, the person guilty of this crime must confront him or suffer a great curse. The goat owner did as Mama Lion had ordered him. Three days passed and nothing happened, so the people started to question her power. Some suggested that maybe old age had weakened her *juju.* Then it happened, on the first Sunday of the new month when the thief was exposed.

"No farmwork is planned on Sundays so people visit each other.

---

7 An imaginary sea creature with the head and upper body of a beautiful woman and the tail of a fish, (a mermaid)
8 A small antelope

That Sunday afternoon, Nokole, a preeminent member of the village, was sitting in his compound with visiting relatives. The day was bright and free from clouds. Birds were chirping happy tunes to everyone's liking, children played happily, chasing each other around in the yard. All the men sat in companies, recounting past events for those who missed them. The women were ⁹combing one another's hair. Then, out of nowhere, a flame shot across the sky. The lightning came directly to Nokole, who was lying in his hammock, and stabbed him in his stomach. Nokole fell out of his hammock and died, instantly. Those who witnessed the unlikely event said that Nokole had been punished for stealing his neighbor's goat. Such untimely incident could only have happened to a guilty person. The old woman's juju had worked once more!

"The people praised the old woman, but only up to the time that Oluma accused her of Momolu's death. You see, Momolu was a celebrity drummer in the village. Rhythm from his drums found way into the bodies of his people and they danced to great satisfaction. When Momolu died, this pleasure in their souls was missed and they grieved deeply. However, their fear of Phephena, though accused, prevented a trial. They stopped using Mama Lion's juju in solving crimes and many even refused her herbs for their healing. Before long, people were no longer afraid of her nor did they respect her.

"Then, on the first morning of the new hunting season, ten hunters entered the village with a curious uproar. Many ran out of their huts to see the reason for the commotion. What the people witnessed that day had never seemed possible. The old medicine woman, whose thrilling juju had in fact paralyzed the villagers with fear, was now standing helpless with both hands tied behind her back. The hunters pushed and shoved Phephena around with no concern, while they argued her fate.

"'Let the man who witnessed the crime come to tell us,' said one of the hunters. However, each time when Oluma was sent for, he refused. He did not believe that Mama Lion had lost her juju powers and wanted no part of their mock trial. But the hunters insisted on Oluma's testimony until he came unwillingly.

"Oluma retold the story about *Mammy-water* saving him and rewarding him with riches. He later suggested that Phephena is put to

---

9 *Plaiting or braiding hair*

death; otherwise, they all would be cursed as Momolu was.

"Although Oluma had said all those things about Phephena, she did not defend her innocence. So quarrels among the men continued with no gain. Then, Todi (*toe-dee*), an old councilor in the village, saw there would be no progress in a disorderly trial. He raised the point and argued that Phephena ought to defend herself. At first, Todi's plead went in vain but he continued until it was agreed. The hunters forced Phephena into confession, threatening her with a harsh punishment. Then, the old woman had no choice, so she decided to tell her story.

"One night while gathering herbs, she heard the fall of footsteps near the creek. She thought they were hunters, so she stopped collecting herbs and hid behind the bushes. In a little while, two men showed up. They chatted while one man tied a rope around his waist and was later lowered into the creek with the help of his friend. After some time, his friend pulled him out of the water with a bucket in his hand. Phephena did not see a bucket in his hand when the man was lowered into the creek, but he came up with one.

"They chatted some more. Only this time, their whispers changed into an argument and soon intensified into a quarrel. Then, the old woman thought it wise to leave the creek. She hurried home and told her husband what she had witnessed. The next morning, Momolu's body was found near the creek, mutilated. Her husband warned her not to disclose what she had witnessed and advised that it would bring trouble to their home, so Phephena heeded to his warning.

"Oluma continuously interrupted the old woman while she told her story. Each time he interrupted, Todi begged for his silence. But Oluma's argument grew more harshly. Then one hunter suggested that Phephena's husband come to confirm her story. But, her husband had died a year after the incident. In that case, Phephena had no choice but to reveal the long kept secret of the creek. She disclosed to the people about the diamonds that were buried in the creek.

"You see, the story about the diamonds was considered rumor. Many years before, it was decided, on the advice of the village chief, the leaders kept it secret until the time of hardship. By that time, the diamonds were to be divided among the people. The leaders renamed the creek, Sugar Creek, without telling the people the meaning behind the name.

"Todi, being one of two elders in the village, knew about the diamonds. He confirmed the old woman's story, but did so unwillingly. Had it not been for the sake of the old woman's life, Todi would have rather taken that secret to his grave. Nevertheless, Oluma's argument became so vigorous that spiteful arguments intensified among the hunters. While disagreements and suggestions went unsettled, Oluma was asked repeatedly, 'How did Mama Lion do her magic that night? Why didn't the mermaid also help Momolu?' Oluma changed his answers many times until finally, realizing he was losing his ground, he confessed his crime.

"It happened that Oluma's grandfather was not a hard worker, his strength was to sit still every day. Because he could not leave much to his family after his death, he told Oluma about the diamonds and advised him to take some of the diamonds and share it with the family. Oluma planned the robbery soon after his grandfather's death. He was not able to steal the diamonds by himself because of the river depth, so he confided his plan in Momolu, his best friend and the two men became partners in the crime.

"It was greed that propelled Momolu into deeper deceit. While he was at the bottom of the creek collecting the diamonds, he thought it wise to swallow a few pieces. Oluma suspected Momolu when he came out of the creek and questioned his friend's loyalty. That created tension between the friends. They began an argument which later turned into a violent struggle. It was during their scuffle that Momolu hit his head on a rock and died. Oluma panicked, and because he did not want to carry the blame, he told the villagers that Mama Lion's evil spell had punished Momolu for no clear reason.

"After Oluma's confession, the hunters freed Phephena. Later that day, the village chief and councilors assembled in the palava hut for Oluma's trial. Oluma's possessions were taken away and according to their judgment, he was sentenced to spend the rest of his life in prison. Phephena was offered a compensation for her troubles, but the old woman refused it. She wanted none of Oluma's blood money. Momolu's father was awarded Oluma's belongings–his land, sheep, goats and huts. The diamonds were divided among the members of the village as each was given his equal share."

Oldman Jallah then ended his story with a parable.

"My little children, it is easy to tell a lie, but it is hard to tell just *one* lie. No matter what the situation, the law of justice is sure," he said, and winked his eye as he caught the attention of each child. Their little mouths went from innocent smiles to pleasant childish giggles.

It was time to go home and the children got up as if they did not care to go back to their homes. Some pleaded to hear more stories, but Oldman Jallah promised that a new story will be told on the follow evening. He had always kept the better story for the following evening.

Normally pairing best friend with best friend and baby-siblings with their older siblings, the group of children left Oldman Jallah's kitchen and went walking back to their homes. He could not help but grin at their silly arguments as some tried retelling the story, even mimicking his tone of voice.

When he could no longer see the children, Oldman Jallah got up, cleaned all the things that he had used during the day and put them away in their usual spots. He filled his kerosene lantern with oil, held a piece of dried stick against the burning coal, blew it into flames, and lit the wick on his lantern. Holding the lantern waist high, he checked the kitchen to make sure that everything was left in its proper place. Then he sprinkled water on the [10]*fire* and waited for the coals to sizzle cold. Oldman Jallah inspected the kitchen once more before going to his bedroom.

There was no table or bed or any other furniture in his hut except the straw mat, rolled up and placed against the mud wall. Oldman Jallah put down his lantern, took the mat, and spread it open in the middle of his empty hut. Any other person would have enjoyed the beauty of the graceful moonlight rather than the need to sleep. However, the old man lowered the wick to low beam setting and lied down quietly on his mat. Like every other night, he begged sleep to help him forget his loss, but it was long in coming. At some time pass midnight, Oldman Jallah dozed off.

Like many mornings before, he woke up at dawn to the cries of the pepper birds.

---

10 *A three-stoned hearth built for cooking*

THE DOWRY OF VIRGINS

L ife was pleasant in Twoku Village until an ugly gossip started about the daughter of an important elder that had been defiled. There would be no report of firing gunshots on the night of her wedding to show that she is a virgin and has pleased her husband. Worst, she was with child and the child did not belong to the man to whom she was engaged. In the old days, evil was to be put out of the village and the man and woman were put to death because they had given their families a bad name.

Twoku Village had thirty huts closely packed together in no clear order, except for a few that were made of family of rank groups. Most of the huts are formed with a framework of light poles interwoven with thin branches and the walls are filled with mud and then plastered with smooth clay taken from abandoned [1]bug-a-bug mounts. Most hut roofs are covered with palm [2]thatch except those families with some rank. Their huts are built rectangular shape with several rooms, a porch and, in Josef Yeke's case, a zinc roof.

Josef Yeke was clothed with some power of sort. Although he was not one of royalty, he sat among the lawgivers of his village; one of the twelve head elders who dipped their hands in the kola nut bowl to fulfill justice among the people.

He loved his seven children, especially his daughters who sat down at his feet every evening after supper to receive his words in tales and parables. If it was left to him, his three daughters would remain between

---

1 *Mount created by large termite (ants). Such mount can reach a height of an eight to ten feet hall and have the strength of hard clay or cement*
2 *Whole palm branches are folded over and stitched closely together into bands; one band is laid on top of another to make double thickness of palm branches. The folded palm branches are placed like shingles*

his shoulders always to keep them safe. Josef Yeke decided when it came to marriage he would not do his sons' choosing. They will marry whom they thought best, as long as the women were from their tribe. His daughters on the other hand, he would make top priority in selecting men who will bring honor to the family's name.

The youngest of his three daughters, Nyawa, was the apple of her father's eye. Now finding out about Nyawa's unwed pregnancy, Josef Yeke's hopes and fears for his daughters met on the same day. After five months of hiding, the baby had taken on a life of its own in her belly. Mayray Yeke knew of her daughter's pregnancy long before everyone, although Nyawa did not admit to it or named the baby's father when her mother approached her. Kaimu made the confession through the words of Oldman Jallah, Josef Yeke's oldest and dearest friend, but only to the young woman's father.

The morning sun hung as low as his spirits. The dry season air hazed like a blanket, covering the freshness of the morning. Josef Yeke's soul grieved for the misery of his daughter as he sat in the sitting area of his hut alone, waiting on his guests and trying hard to put the best face on the matter to make his behavior seem normal. When his guests arrive, they must meet him with a fresh spirit. But these were no ordinary guests. One was the man accused of stealing his daughter's virginity and the other, an old friend, whose support was equally divided between the accused and the accuser.

"Josef, if this is too hard for you, take it to the Chief so he hears it," his wife advised.

Mayray Yeke had come to tell him the food and drinks were ready for his guests, as he had requested. She made sure none of the things Kaimu sent was used. Her husband made that clear at the time of delivery.

"My dear wife," he said, "I have heard cases between strangers and brothers. I have judged rightly between everyone and his accuser. I do not respect the rank of people in my judgments, but hear the ordinary man as well as the great man. Do you think I am afraid in the face of any man?"

Mayray Yeke smiled. "In none of those trials had anyone touched your precious Nyawa," she muttered.

Josef Yeke chose to ignore those remarks.

Mayray Yeke left her husband, only to come back twenty minutes later to let him know the men had arrived. She stuck her head through the door and whispered, "They're here."

"We will sit in here," Josef Yeke told her. "Do not serve the food and drinks until I call you."

She nodded and left.

Josef Yeke greeted the men at the door, escorted them to his sitting area, and pointed at the three stools arranged in a circle that he had prepared for their comfort. Oldman Jallah slowly lowered his aged body on one bench and laid his walking stick by his foot. Kaimu sat quietly, like a bag of nerves, until he had adjusted to all the movements and sounds of Josef Yeke and his staring. The three men sat with the understanding that during their conversation, although unofficial, the rule of uninterrupted speaking was to be applied. In addition, for the sake of good etiquette, to begin a conversation by moving directly to the issue is not considered proper. He who does so is selfish; he does not care for the other person, only for the business at hand. Oldman Jallah and Kaimu waited patiently for Josef Yeke to start since they were his guests.

"Is life treating you well?" Josef Yeke greeted his guests.

"I praise God!" Oldman Jallah said. "Life treats me as well as any old man. My body is frail so I do not move about as before, but I still get around."

"I'm well," Kaimu muttered.

"Good...good," Josef Yeke said and moved right to the point. "Oldman Jallah, you are my good friend and we have known each other for many years. Such a case should be brought before the elders, but I've invited Kaimu here at your request rather than go to the Chief and village councils. If a man is convicted of adultery with another man's wife, we know he has to pay, to that man, a larger fine than the dowry collected. If an engaged young woman was no longer a virgin, she would be compelled to identify the man with whom she had had sex and she is stripped of her dignity. All the people in the village dishonor her. This love that Kaimu has, is it so amazing that it demands my daughter's pride? Nyawa is my last child. I see her as my richest gain because I had her in my old age. I nearly lost Mayray, my dear wife. Now that sorrow and love mingle, should I count Nyawa as loss because it pours disrespect on her name? I am deeply wounded with this disgrace. How can I lift my face when shame weighs down my head so heavily?"

Josef Yeke collected his thoughts for a minute or two. He had not finished and did not expect anyone to talk. No one spoke a word.

"Forgive me if I should sound as if I am boasting, I am not," Josef Yeke continued. "God is my witness, as I have lived more than seventy years in Twoku. Everybody knows that I have kept my oath, even when it hurt. I have never accepted a bribe against anyone. I have always spoken the truth from my heart. I have never created a slander on my tongue against anyone. I have envied no one. All my life, I have tried to do no wrong at will. My wife will tell you, I do my best to leave rage aside. Still, evil has found its way to my house. What must a man do in life to enjoy untroubled peace? Why has Kaimu targeted my daughter, as if she has no name? How can he pay what he does not have? How can a palm-wine tapper be a benefit to my daughter? What insurance can he give in my daughter's welfare? What can Nyawa gain even if Kaimu was blameless?"

Josef Yeke heaved a sigh and muttered, "I will speak the truth that is in my heart. When I look at the man that dishonored me, my heart beats restlessly in my chest. You are aware of how we live in this village. Since the beginning of time, a man interested in a woman must first speak with her father. Nyawa has already been spoken for, so Kaimu had no rights to her!"

Josef Yeke finished and sat quietly.

After a little while, when Kaimu felt it was time to talk, he cleared his throat and addressed his accuser.

"Oldman Yeke, I love your daughter," Kaimu said. "It is only love that has put me on this road. If I had asked for your listening ears, to engage Nyawa, would you have given it?"

"Wait!" Oldman Jallah interrupted Kaimu, sensing that because of Kaimu's young mind, he had started foolishly. He thought wisely the best time to stop an argument is before it starts. "You two must not argue with empty words," he suggested. "Your words must have value."

Kaimu nodded and thought it best to end his speech. "You are right," he said to Oldman Jallah.

"Kaimu, if Josef Yeke hold you to even a greater debt, he is right," Oldman Jallah said. "Your own words condemn you and we are all witnesses to it." Then he turned to Josef Yeke and said, "Kaimu's lips testified against him, but Kaimu is not the first man to know love and limit it to his own selfishness. What does Kaimu know about love that we old men do not know? Even as gray hair is on my side, I was not born before the mountains…to see love as Kaimu have seen it. In Kaimu's search for love, he has used deceit as easy as a man drinks water." He then turned to Kaimu. "That, my son, is not the way you approach love," he said. "If you had done the proper thing, would you not have been accepted? When temptation knocked at your door, like the desire that seemed yours, you should have ruled over it. You allowed it to rule over you. Open rebuke is far better than secret love. Love is not love until it is given openly, even when none seem well."

Kaimu nodded.

Oldman Jallah turned to Josef Yeke.

"And you, my good friend," he said, "We have been friends for many years."

"Yes," Josef Yeke agreed.

"We have seen many things," Oldman Jallah continued. "We know that when all seems good, we do not let it fool us. No one knows when the bad times are coming. Trouble was not made for only certain people or certain time. Trouble follows all. Furthermore, God makes it possible for a man to put an end to his poverty. A man's hand changes his worth by those things God has placed everywhere. The mine has silver and gold in it. The same ground where we get our food, iron is taken from the earth. The river where we get drinking water also feeds us with fish. The foot of this man," he pointed at Kaimu, "can take him to those places. So Josef Yeke, do not flaunt your riches or shake your fist against him when he is swallowed in poverty and trouble. His face has already been covered with shame. Josef Yeke must not think his good name and wealth, which spreads throughout this village and beyond, is to last forever. Be truthful to yourself, my good friend. The value of anything is worthless, until it has a use. What good is a canoe if there is no water?"

Josef Yeke furrowed his brow. "If you were in my shoes, do you think fine speeches will cool your heart?" He rebutted immediately. "Will comforting words give you relief? This man has disgraced my entire family, but witnessing Kaimu die of shame will not send my shame away. The best inheritance a man can leave his children is a life lived with integrity. What does Kaimu have? Because of him, my daughter's life speaks against me. This will not go away for my other two daughters. Men will always question their honor. Kaimu has bound my household. It was Kaimu who went looking for quarrel against me. All was well with me, until he did this ugly thing. I feel as if Kaimu has deliberately placed his foot on my neck to crush me. These days, I walk in my own yard with my head hanging. Even my old eyes have leaked tears. Yet, my hands will remain free of violence against him. God is my witness; I have planned no evil against Kaimu."

Josef Yeke sighed.

"My spirit is broken," he continued. "I know my hurt can only be cured by some years that are to pass. Even my few days left in me will be hard. Today, my grave seems a better place. Kaimu has made me to look simple in everyone's eye. You are a wise man Jallah...tell Kaimu how he is to bring honor back to my house. Even you, the wisest old man in Twoku Village, cannot do it. Only God can turn night into day. So, show me Jallah, where is my family's hope?"

"When you put an end to your harsh words of hopelessness," Oldman Jallah said, pointing to his own heart. "Why does living seem worthless when life is still in you? Your anger will rip you to pieces," he pointed at Josef Yeke. "When that happens, should Kaimu and Nyawa also abandon living? Nothing last forever, Yeke, you know that. The flames of these fires too will stop burning. Their gossips will weaken with time. Where there is a will, there is always a way. Now that Kaimu has disturbed his neighbor's life, must destruction be the solution? Josef Yeke, you are one of the twelve wise men in Twoku Village, you can find a way to work this thing out."

After breathing fire for a full hour, the three men drank the water Mayray Yeke had put near each bench.

"Who in this village can be found honorable always in his life or blameless always when he is accused?" Kaimu said, as soon as his cup left his lips. "Who in Twoku Village have not seen my mistake? Everyone treats me harshly. It is because I am not innocent. It is my fault, Oldman Yeke, allowing things to simmer for a while. I've waited too long to come to face you. I wanted the stew to be right, but waiting six months was too long. I am guilty and I am not scared of speaking what is in my heart. I love your daughter. Tell me what charges you have against me, so I humble myself in front of all and beg your pardon. I am not asking to go unpunished. Punish me, so I can lift my head again and show my face. Inside my body, I am a dying man."

"Am I being forced to give my answer now?" Josef Yeke asked angrily. "Am I to say all that is in my heart? Well, Kaimu, the consequences of your deceit is small compare with my daughter's shame. Nyawa's shame is deep. Her life can no longer be as bright as I would have liked it. She can only lay down with the man who has stolen her honor. For the rest of her life, many will see her shame. There's no escape in that!"

"I am willing to die because of it!" Kaimu shouted, and then he lowered his voice and said, "I am not afraid of that. Becoming a laughingstock to my people has not shamed me enough. I look at those who carry their good name in their own mouths and do not wait for others to speak it. I would like to ask them; who owns a blameless life? I cannot...because of my own guilt. Old people are wise because long life brings understanding, so I pray that you will see my deceit for what it is. Let your wisdom teach me. Let my ears eat your words as my tongue taste food. Only God knows the hearts of both the deceived and the deceiver. God knows the reason I have put my life into such jeopardy. Although I have dishonored your daughter, God knows I speak the truth when I say that I love her. My foolishness has made love seem a grave mistake, by stealing her honor."

Kaimu got up, lowered his body, and held Josef Yeke's feet.

"Oldman Yeke, I am begging you. I can only defend my ways in your face by [3]touching your foot. I have told you what is buried in my heart. I hope your ears will hear me."

Josef Yeke tied his face with discontent.

"Only you can bring charges against me," Kaimu said, and got up. He sat on his bench. "Please, don't let me waste away because of your anger. It will not make your daughter pure again. Even if I die, Nyawa will not become pure again. I am begging you to give Nyawa and I hope instead."

All could see that Josef Yeke's heart was inflamed with anger fire. He sat heavily on his bench. His chest rose and fell with the rhythm of furious breathing.

---

3 *A form of humbleness*

"What are you waiting for?" Oldman Jallah asked Josef Yeke. "Why would you not set judgment? Have you not waited long enough for this opportunity? All power is in your hand, my friend. Charge Kaimu with the wrong he has done and make your judgment."

"I am at your mercy," Kaimu pleaded. "You have offered your wisdom and I have swallowed it. All power is in your hands, so let God touch your heart before you deal with me. Please, do not deny me justice so my enemies laugh at me. What place will I have among my people if I am cut off? Teach me the power of mercy. Do not let my words go unheard or become meaningless. I promise to love Nyawa as long as I have life in me."

"You are not good enough for my daughter!" Josef Yeke shouted, angrily.

There was long silence before Josef Yeke spoke again.

"What difference will it make, Kaimu? The way a man's love accommodates his wife brings respect to her. You have done the opposite. Marriage thrives in a climate of love and respect...not only love. A priority for the husband to become a head of his wife is to know and understand her family...that it may go well with him. Without that commitment, a man is not capable of doing what comes next, which is honoring her. You are not good enough for my Nyawa!" Josef Yeke said, shaking his head.

"If you would not allow the two to get married, what will happen to your daughter?" Oldman Jallah asked.

"I will send her to her mother's people," Josef Yeke replied, with a cold hearted voice.

"What about the baby?" Oldman Jallah asked.

Josef Yeke looked at Kaimu. "Nyawa does not have a husband, so the baby belongs to her," he replied. "It makes no difference."

Kaimu swallowed his saliva hard. His heart melted as if there was no spirit left in him, knowing another man could raise his child. Nearing the end of his rope, he found his courage and stood up.

"How long will your words flog me?" Kaimu said to Josef Yeke. "How hard are you willing to crush me to the ground? You have used your rank and age to attack me. If you meant to use humiliation to scorn me, you have used it well. I have begged you. I have cried my heart out, yet you will not lay your justice on me. Will Josef Yeke continue to count me among his enemies?"

Josef Yeke chuckled sarcastically. "We have not assembled here as friends," he said sharply. "Have you forgotten?"

"How can I forget?" Kaimu said.

"Then, who are you to question my chastening?" Josef Yeke rebutted.

To stop things from getting out of hand, Oldman Jallah felt the need to intervene.

"Josef Yeke, do not let this day be of sorrow because you're in a revengeful frame of mind," Oldman Jallah said. "Your attitude is choking the life out of Kaimu. Do not hate him to the point where your heart is hardened."

"Can't I ask, for the sake of my daughter's welfare, without fingers pointed at me?" Josef Yeke questioned his old friend's loyalty. It was irritating to hear his longtime friend defend his enemy. "To defile a man's daughter, is it not wickedness? What have I done in comparison to Kaimu? Kaimu demands respect from me when he has not given any. Love is not bad. Stirring it up with deceit is. He talks as if I am rejoicing in his troubles. It is my daughter's trouble and her troubles are my trouble. Kaimu must restore honor to him before he can restore honor to my daughter. I cannot do that for him. I refuse to lift Kaimu on the shoulders of giants. He has to restore his own honor!"

"My hands are tied," Kaimu said, raising both his hands. "This thing has alienated me from my friends, to the point that I have no guests coming to my house. No one is willing to show his face around my place. Even a ⁴pekin will not listen to me these days. My own family has turned against me. Look at me...I am nothing but skin and bones. My only escape is by your pity. Oldman Yeke, have pity on this fool which love has used foolishly. I love Nyawa and I want to grow old with her."

"Did you not hear me?" Josef Yeke snarled. "You are not good enough for my daughter!"

"I deserve every word that is spoken against me," Kaimu said, shaking his head. "I may not seem as much in your eyes because my family has no status in Twoku Village. When I die and you die, our bodies would be cover with the earth. Will the worms prefer one to another? Which reason hurts you more? Is it that I've paid no money to your account or I have no status? In your court, a wicked man can

---

4 *A young boy (preteen & teenager)*

be spared from his ways. Can a poor man also be spared? Without money, I should have come to you earlier and stated my deeds. At least I would have known your answer. Would you have condemned me? Would you have judged me according to my family's name or by my character? Had I done it, I would not be sitting here pleading with my pride to be delivered from your judgment. Would I have found fairness or respect? Would I have found favor in your eyes?"

Kaimu covered his chest with both hands and added, "I was a coward before coming here. I know now the way I should have taken, but how do I convince you that I treasure your daughter more than food? I do not have money or fame, but I have good plans in store for us. I will tell you how a palm-wine tapper will be a benefit to your daughter. I love Nyawa, to the point where I have silence my voice toward every other woman. I will be gracious to her should she become my wife. If my words are not honored, let God curse me. Let others eat what I've sown. May my corps be uprooted by the groundhogs. Let my dear Nyawa cook another man his meal and let him sleep with her instead of me...which will kill me. Let God confront me so my answer is to Him, because man cannot destroy me as well as God can. I swear...I will never go back on my words. Oldman Yeke, I will never become unfaithful to Nyawa. Should this not go in my favor, people will mock me. Shame will become my clothing. It will bring me down sooner than later...even closer to death. Josef Yeke...I am begging you."

Oldman Jallah looked at his friend; Josef Yeke caught his stare.

"What would you gain by denying Kaimu your daughter's hand in marriage?" Oldman Jallah asked.

"Hear my answer, Jallah," Josef Yeke replied hastily. "I have every right to be bitter under these circumstances, but I cannot allow bitterness to control me or taint my life in any way. I do not want bitterness to overshadow my good name. God will heal the hurt that Kaimu has caused my family. He brought up an evil name on my daughter, a virgin in my house. He made Nyawa to play a whore in her father's house. By our customs, he is to pay me one hundred pieces of silver. He does not own a single piece of silver in his name. In the old days, a man is put to death for this, so evil is put out of the village. These days, people pay money for their evil deeds. What happens if the man has no money? Should he labor like an animal? Would it matter if he becomes my woodcutter or my water pot carrier? His presence will only remind me of the evil he has planted. See, my hands are also tied. No other man will want my daughter and this one cannot afford her. Am I to throw my daughter away to the wind?"

"Certainly not," Oldman Jallah replied. "That is not what I am asking."

"This man obeyed the needs of his natural self and my daughter has to pay for it," Josef Yeke continued. "Had he waited patiently, this love that he talks about would not have passed his misunderstanding. Kaimu knows better. Today shame and sorrow opens my door because of him. Why, have Kaimu treated my daughter so? How do you expect me to show mercy with cheerfulness, especially to the man that defiled my Nyawa?"

"Do it for your daughter's sake," Oldman Jallah said, calmly. "Love is much more than feelings. It is a lifelong commitment. Kill the hate that is in you, Josef Yeke, so good can come back to your house. No good will come to the unforgiving heart as long as it continues to breed bad feelings. Let the bitterness go. No one is free from debt, not even you and I. Debt does not always have the face of money. Our greatest debt that we have is to God. God gives to all, the rich, the poor, the young, the old, the ordinary man and the great man. Kaimu has come to seek forgiveness. Settle with him today so your family can have peace. If you wipe away the tears of your enemy, it is God who will wipe away yours."

Josef Yeke sighed. "Since when did the dowry of virgins become so worthless?" he asked. "Where was Kaimu when I was wiping Mayray Yeke's brow, when the labor pain gave her no mercy? Where was he when I was bringing up my daughters, who sat at my feet since they were infants? Are his plans for my daughter better than my own? He has no children, so how can he know the pain of a father? Has Kaimu fed any other person, day after day, other than himself? Has he made farms beyond his own needs for the sake of others? Has he gone to bed hungry so his little ones are fed first? Correct me, if I am wrong. Let Kaimu tell me those answers."

"I deserve every word that is spoken against me here," Kaimu said. "I will not speak another word. My lips are sealed," he cupped his hand and covered his mouth.

"Remove your hand from your mouth," Oldman Jallah ordered.

"Accept his condemnation for wrongfully dishonoring his daughter. Accept his corrections!"

Kaimu immediately removed his hand. "His heart will not pity me," he muttered. "How can I put away my guilt? He did not need two or three witnesses to speak against me. I am the only witness to do so. My own lips have been my accuser. I am begging Oldman Yeke for pity. Please, let your pity drive away all anger and hate. Let things be new between us."

Hearing the fall of footsteps near his door, Josef Yeke raised his palm to hush Kaimu from speaking. He got up and walked to his door to see the intruder.

"Kwolli (*qill-lee*) has come," Mayray Yeke told her husband as she approached the door with a twenty-something year old man. She left the men and returned to attend her own business.

"Hello, Uncle Josef," the young man greeted, extending his hand.

They shook hand and Josef Yeke invited him in with a slow wave.

"Kwolli is the son of my wife's oldest brother," Josef Yeke introduced his nephew to his guests, and then asked, "What brings you all the way from Ganta?"

Seeing his uncle's guests, Kwolli hesitated to speak his mind freely. It did not seem right to out the family's business that had brought him two hundred miles.

"You can talk," Josef Yeke gave the go-ahead.

"We have found the man for Nyawa," Kwolli whispered so only his uncle's ears would catch the message.

"Good," Josef Yeke replied and added, "Get a stool and join us."

Kwolli left and, returned with a bench. He placed it near his uncle, shook hands with his uncle's guests and sat quietly.

"Let me ask you, Oldman Yeke," Kaimu brought the business back to focus. "What can I do to make things right?"

"This is the man that spoiled Nyawa," Josef Yeke said to Kwolli, while pointing at Kaimu. "Now he wants forgiveness. Is it not adding drunkenness to thirst? He defiled my daughter and now he wants to be my son. Can you draw freshwater and saltwater from the same well?"

"No," Kwolli replied and added respectfully, "No creek will give both saltwater and freshwater."

"I love Nyawa," Kaimu mumbled.

"He loves Nyawa, but dishonors her," Josef Yeke mocked.

Kwolli wanted to hear more, he chose not to reply.

"Mind your words," Oldman Jallah advised Josef Yeke. "Remember, [5]you cannot unsneeze a sneeze. A root of bitterness will bring trouble in the future. If you do not listen to me, good will reject your house. This man is begging you with his tears. Will his begging only be heard if in the company of great men? Bear in mind, the spirit of a man is not perfect in the presence of *any* woman. His way of approaching this love may not be speaking better things than his heart, but you must hear him. Kaimu loves your daughter. Although you have every right to be bitter, do not refuse him when he speaks. Forgiveness must not wait too long."

"Kaimu is not innocent," Josef Yeke pointed out. "What he has done to me is unthinkable. I have the power to see him dead, but have I directed my voice there?"

"No...thank God!" Oldman Jallah replied.

"So, why does it seem that judgment is pointing at me? It is Kaimu who has ruined my life."

"I am not pointing judgment at you," Oldman Jallah corrected. "I am advising you to choose your words carefully. Season your words with the balm of forgiveness, not with the poison of anger. You have measured your pride in personal achievements rather than your good character. Josef Yeke, I've known you personally for many years. You are a good man. You know that a man's character is far more important than his achievements. When you measure this man's worth by your own worth, it is not wise. Recognize the hypocrisy here. Those who see the faults in another man's life are often what are true in his own life. Your judgment must not be based on material things which are here today and gone tomorrow. What's important is we must live honorably with other people daily. Do you think your daughter have settled for less by marrying a man whose family has no status or money?"

Oldman Jallah waited for Josef Yeke to respond, but he remained silent.

Oldman Jallah asked, "Why is it that in our culture, the compassion of the rich and famous disappears as soon as their heads rise above the level of their brothers? Stop mourning your daughter's

---

5 *African parable - one cannot take back what has been said or done*

virginity, to the point of vengeance. You have grieved long enough. Dress your heart with forgiveness instead of ashes of hate. Welcome Kaimu among your sons instead of meeting him with despair. He has opened his own mouth against him. If Kaimu goes back on his word, let God deal with him. I believe Kaimu will live according to the words he has spoken."

"Let my nephew speak while I think," Josef Yeke suggested.

"Thank you, Uncle Josef," Kwolli jumped in. "I am younger than the three of you here, and for the sake of respect, I will use my words with caution. However, I will flatter none of you. My words come from my heart, so my lips will speak truthfully. God is my witness."

"Talk," Josef Yeke muttered, being aware of his nephew's philosophized spirit.

"Oldman Jallah and Uncle Josef are older and wiser, so they have the understanding of many things," Kwolli said. "However, it is not only the old people that are wise and know what is right. I have sat here and patiently listened to your words of reasoning. I have not heard anything mentioned on Nyawa's behalf or spoken in her favor."

All three men frowned on Kwolli's scrutiny.

"My spirit in me compels me to speak on her behalf," Kwolli defended his position.

Josef Yeke chuckled to his nephew's frankness.

"My uncle condemns Kaimu of doing wrong to him, but all wrong has been done to Nyawa, not him," Kwolli continued. "Kaimu has taken Nyawa's honor and blames love. He justifies it with his plan and complaints of how people are treating him, not Nyawa. What about her shame? Today, Nyawa is suffering with the sickness of shame. Where is the balm for her? These days can she go to the creek to draw water without the others looking down at her?"

Then Kwolli turned to Oldman Jallah and said, "Oldman Jallah, too, has had his sayings. He is seeking good judgment on behalf of his young friend. I, for one, will speak on Nyawa's behalf."

The three men sat straighter, immersed in the young man's preaching.

"Kaimu, you are wrong for stealing Nyawa's honor," Kwolli said to Kaimu. "Still, it is good that pride has not kept you away. You have come to my uncle and humbled yourself. Have you gone to Nyawa to beg her for forgiveness? If there is true remorse in you, you must ask

Nyawa to forgive you. Let her see your face and become happy, rather than hang her head. Beg for her pardon in public, not in private. This will redeem her from shame. It is Nyawa, not any of you, who is the laughingstock in Twoku Village."

"I will do that," Kaimu said. "That is easy for me to do."

"The man we have found for Nyawa is a good man, but he is not good for her," Kwolli continued. "He is an old man and thinks the baby will make him young. That is the main reason he is willing to take her. He will not love Nyawa as Kaimu would. Nyawa has suffered the pain of abandonment for six months, which is too long for heart troubles. Our people have concerns for her, but they will not give her the hope of healing. Only a caring husband can do that for her. He can lift her burden of shame."

"Are you finished?" Josef Yeke asked.

Kwolli nodded. He had more to say, but thought it wise to stop this far. Most of his points, intended for Kaimu especially, had been made.

"Kwolli, you are wise for your age," Oldman Jallah said, pointing at him, smiling. "I would not have thought of those things that you've said, even with gray hair on my side. We are men with gray hairs, but we are not gods."

"Kwolli is a small boy, but he sits among men," Josef Yeke bragged. "In our culture, [6]a pekin with clean hands eats with kings.

"Yes," Kaimu agreed.

"He has the soul of an old man," Oldman Jallah complimented and went back to the business at hand. "Josef Yeke, we have heard the boy, so what do you have to say?"

Josef Yeke pondered for a moment.

"If I give to Kaimu my blessings, I must also curse him," he replied.

"Only God can do such things," Oldman Jallah advised. "Why would you want to do God's work? Are you saying that God owes you a favor? God does not give His glory to another."

"God does not owe me a favor," Josef Yeke replied quickly. "Who owes God anything? God *is* God!"

"Then my good friend, recognize what God has put before you,"

---

6 *African parable - a young person that shows maturity and self-respect is allowed to sit among adults.*

Oldman Jallah said. "Good and evil are before you for a reason. The one you must choose is in your heart. No one has to go across the river for the right one, to bring it to you, that you may hear it and do it. Blessing and curse sits before you. Choose what is in your heart."

Josef Yeke sat quietly to consider his decision.

"Choose well my friend, so God can bless you and your children," Oldman Jallah added.

"Sometimes it is better to bite your tongue," Josef Yeke said instead.

"What are you saying? Are you not going to pass judgment?" Oldman Jallah asked.

"I will pass judgment," Josef Yeke said, "but you must hear me first."

Oldman Jallah nodded.

"The tongue is small and it boasts of big things," Josef Yeke said. "We men tame wild animals, but we cannot tame our own tongue. We have all heard Kaimu speaks of his love for my daughter, 'I love Nyawa, Oldman Yeke, I love your daughter'. He has said it repeatedly. Only when his actions show it, then [7]my heart will sit down. Until that time comes, if Kaimu should treat my daughter immorally in any way, his life will be cursed by his own lips. God will lay hands on him so others will always stand above him. He will always be a borrower rather than a lender. Other people will eat his labor. His sons will turn their backs on him to honor another man. If Kaimu treats Nyawa immorally, God will give him a trembling heart. Kaimu will go down low, to become the tail in the village. Do not fear me Kaimu...fear God. I am sure these will come true should you go back on your words."

"It is God whom I fear most," Kaimu said. "Why would I go back on my words?"

"A man grows old and his eyes become dim," Josef Yeke continued. "His natural strength fades away. Today, if I was younger, I would have used my own hands to squeeze the life out of Kaimu. I thank God that age have given me wisdom and understanding."

Josef Yeke pointed at his old friend to let him know that he was finished. Oldman Jallah now had the opportunity to finish his case.

"Kaimu, whatever that came out of your mouth must be kept,"

---

7 *Liberian expression of satisfaction*

Oldman Jallah said. "Marriage is much more than feelings, it is a life-long commitment. When the time comes and your feelings toward this woman grow cold, you cannot put her away. Bear in mind, the man that you will become, a good name must be given to your wife. No actions on your part must cause her shame or bring any criticism on her good name."

"I will cause my wife no harm," Kaimu replied. "The way I love Nyawa, no word can describe it."

"You do not know what tomorrow has," Oldman Jallah pointed out. "Love comes after the marriage. In your case, you have put it otherwise. A husband is expected to love his wife as his own body. For no reasons, other than your wife lying with another man, can you put her out of your home. Only death must separate you. Whether you are ready or not, your actions have chosen this lifelong commitment."

"I am ready!" Kaimu said. "I do not care what tomorrow may bring."

Oldman Jallah and Josef Yeke looked at Kaimu and shook their heads. They knew better, youth was blinding Kaimu against reality.

"You have spoken well, my good friend," Josef Yeke addressed his old friend. "I believe God put those words in your mouth. What you have said rests easily on my heart. As for Kaimu, I must admit, it will be a long time before I see him as my son. Today, he stands before me as an accused man. Tomorrow, his sons will stand before me with my blood in them. What am I to do then?"

"You have said a great thing," Oldman Jallah praised his friend. "God will bless you for that."

"It is mainly because Kaimu presented himself in the most humble way," Josef Yeke admitted. "Kaimu did not lie about the wrong that he did. Therefore, I decided not to take him to the Council. I will give Varney back his dowry money that he has paid for Nyawa. Kaimu does not have to pay anything to him, but Kaimu must pay his own to me."

Moved to tears, Kaimu got up and knelt at Josef Yeke's feet. He bowed his face to the ground, while Josef Yeke was still talking, and wept.

"It would not matter now," Josef Yeke said. "Why did you not wait? You would have won my approval...patience wins all things."

Kaimu waited until Josef Yeke touched his back, a gesture of his acceptance, and then he stood up.

"I have heard everything that was said today," Kaimu said. "Old-man Yeke, what dialect can I use to thank you? I will borrow it if I had to. I am sorry to have caused your family a great deal of grief. I will never outlive my sorrow for it. I do not deserve your pity, but I am grateful for it. I will do whatever it takes to give Nyawa pride again. I will do what Kwolli has suggested. Whatever that is required, I will do it."

Josef Yeke nodded to accept Kaimu's promises.

"If I go back on my word, let God deal with me," Kaimu swore, touching his heart. Then he extended his hand.

Acceptance of Kaimu into Josef Yeke's family had not gone beyond recall. Josef Yeke held out his hand to Kaimu's gesture of peace and they shook hands. Then all four men shook hands and snapped fingers.

OBIKAI'S HEART

Nine years had flown by since I was last in my village. When I left Mambo Village, I had no plan of returning there; I was coming home because my mother had sent for me.

The painful incident that led to my hasty departure lingers in my heart as though it all happened yesterday. As the first son of a respectable elder, according to our tradition, I was destined to become a part of the male dominance. I was to follow my father's example in becoming an elder and marrying as many wives as I choose to. Those were my father's wishes; I had my own. I broke our tradition, and in doing so, placed shame on my father's head. Resentful of my behavior, he vowed never to forgive me and then he drove me away from his compound. There was great dignity in my father and he would rather die than give in to anyone. I never hated my father for his harsh punishment; it was because of his pride.

Packed with fear and excitement, my heart pounded forcefully in my chest when the old shuttle bus made the final bend down the dirt road heading into Mambo Village. Father's compound sits to the right as you enter the village, with four dainty mud huts tidily kept. I looked toward the hut my parents share and let out a sigh of relief. Nebo, my younger brother, was in the *kitchen* sitting on a stool and talking to Ma while she stood over the steaming pot, stirring whatever she was cooking. At one time, I sat there eagerly waiting for her to finish cooking.

Pee...pee! Pee...pee!

The tooting horn startled me from my daydream. Ma and Nebo looked toward the packed bus as if they were expecting company. Nebo recognized me sitting in the front seat, jumped off his stool, and ran out to meet us. He ran alongside the bus, holding on to the front passenger door handle as we slow down. As soon as the bus stopped, my door flung open. I jumped out and Nebo was right there.

"Hello Quonah (*ko-na*)!" Nebo greeted, smiling from ear to ear.

He looked down at me to show that he was obviously taller than I was. Only sixteen, my younger brother's voice was even deeper. He clasped his arms around me and gave me a tight squeeze, and then we shook hands.

Kamara, the driver, hurriedly collected our fares and begun unloading suitcases from the top luggage rack to return to his loop-route. Nearly everybody in Mamba Village knew him. Before Kamara started driving, his father, Mr. Chalay, ran Little Lamb routes. Those living in the area were familiar with their slogan, *Little Lamb*, handsomely stenciled in black on both sides of the bus. That was the only thing perfect about that vehicle.

Little Lamb was a miserable bus that had been patched over the years with parts from different makes and models. The old bus groaned as if it had never known a grease gun and for as long as I can remember, Little Lamb had never shown a burst of speed. However, it was the only means of getting to Mamba village. When drivers of newer cars refused to drive through mud holes, dusty hill climbs, plank bridges over-cross, and washout ditches that ran diagonally across the way, Little Lamb took us; packed beyond capacity.

"Which is your luggage…this one or that one?" Nebo pointed at the suitcases to make sure he grabbed the right one.

"I did not bring any…I am going back tonight," I said.

Nebo furrowed his brow. "Are you leaving, tonight?" he asked.

"Little Lamb will take me back on Kamara's last run," I said, reluctantly.

There was a touch of disappointment in his stare, but I made nothing of it. Nebo tapped my shoulder and took the lead towards the kitchen.

"How is Father?" I forced the inquiry.

"Didn't you know that Father is sick?" Nebo asked and slowed his steps.

"No," I muttered.

"The old man has been sick for some time now. All the medicine we have tried has failed. Do you remember Oldman Jusu?"

"The village priest…."

"You remember," Nebo said, somewhat surprised that I still knew important people in the village. "Even his medicine has failed. Nothing has helped Father. You know, Ma has begged him repeatedly to go to the hospital, but he refused. He would rather die than take the white man's medicine. He told Ma that their medicine was only for the white man and Africans ought to stick with their own. You would think that he would heed to his own teachings; [1]*If your enemy speaks the truth, do not say because my enemy spoke it I will not listen*."

Based on Nebo's remarks, I figured Father had not abandoned his old way of thinking.

"Is the white man his enemy?" I said, jokingly.

Nebo laughed. I laughed. He knew what I was feeling, just as I had thought. Our father had not abandoned his old way of thinking.

"I did not know Father was ill," I said. "I would have come sooner. No one told me."

Nebo mumbled something underneath his breath and hurried his steps.

As far as I could tell, my brother had not displayed the slightest form of anger toward me. Truthfully, I did not know whether he knew the dispute between our father and I. I had worried about that for a long time, thinking he would hate me. Now the news of my father's illness became more of a concern than his anger toward me. Ma had sent me word to come home, but she had not mentioned anything about Father's illness. I was happy for the invitation, being the only one offered to me since I was kicked out.

"My son has come home!" Ma sang and danced as we walked into the kitchen. She adjusted her lappa and prepared for an embrace. Then as soon as I reached her, she pulled me between her shoulders.

"Hello, Ma," I hugged her. Then I leaned back to catch her eyes. "Ma...Ma...you look wonderful."

Older women in our village carried themselves with a lesser amount of bother, but our mother always looked stylish–managing her weight, wearing well-pressed lappa, and sporting neat hairdos. She looked more beautiful than when I last saw her. There were laughter wrinkles covering her face in a most beautiful network of creases. Her hair, neatly braided down her neck, had a shiny blackness that shouted *youth*. The years had no bearing on her. I cherished

---

1 *African parable*

my mother's appearance and thought, how selfish of me for wanting my mother to remain young forever.

"Quonah, I have missed you," Ma said, and began inspecting my body. Inch by inch, she moved her eyes from the crown of my head down to my feet. "You did not leave your mother's house skinny, but you have returned looking as if there is no food in the city. Is there any food in the city or not?"

"Ma, in the city, it is the big shots that are fat. I am not a big shot. In fact, I'm not skinny at all, Obikai feeds me well," I added, jovially rubbing my belly. "Speaking of Obikai, here is a picture of your grandson," I pulled the picture out of my shirt pocket and handed it to Ma.

She took the picture and stared at it for a minute or more.

"The boy looks just like you when you were a boy," Ma muttered, with hardly any expression.

She was seeing my family photo for the first time.

"I did not know that I am an uncle," Nebo said and then reached for the photograph.

"You are an uncle," Ma said to Nebo and handed me the picture.

Nebo grabbed the picture before I could. He studied it briefly. "I think that I know this woman," he said. "Is she from our village? Who is she?"

"That is Obikai," I said to him. "Yes, she is from our village."

"That is the woman who...."

Ma did not finish. Though there was no need, she clenched the upper part of her lappa and retucked it into place; her hands were shaking. Nebo looked at her and handed me the picture. I reluctantly accepted it.

"I brought it for you, Ma," I said and handed it back to her.

"Quonah, this is not a good time," Ma said, refusing to take it. "Put it away, put it away...I do not want your father laying eyes on it."

"When is it a good time, Ma, after Obikai dies? Do you hate her too? Father hates her, and that is his affair, not yours. Obikai is the mother of my son!"

"Keep your voice down," Ma cautioned in a whisper. "How can I hate the woman that makes my son happy?"

"It's hard to tell, Ma," I said. "You barely looked at the photograph. Did you not see that Obikai is holding your grandson?"

"Quonah, I do not hate her," Ma said, trying her best to sound convincing. "I hate what happened between you and your father. I am concern that if your father sees the picture, it will only revive bad memories. What am I to do, then? Do you not have one with just the boy in it? Why did you have to bring one with *her* in it? I want you to make things right between you and your father. Please, Quonah, for peace sake!"

I disputed the thoughts in my mind, '*Make right with my father,*' '*Why had I come? Why did I think things had changed?*' I had not been home a full hour and already my eagerness to see my family was changing. As my excitement was disappearing, I stood pouting like a young child.

"Quonah, your father is very sick," Ma stressed. "Did your brother not tell you?"

"I did," Nebo said quickly.

"He did," I confirmed.

"Maybe he is too sick to fight with you now," Ma said. "I wish that he sees you, regardless. Please, Quonah, do it for me."

Hearing the sympathy in her voice evoked the immeasurable love that I have for my mother. I quickly put away my pride and my own anger.

"Okay, Ma," I said calmly, "I will try."

Her dark brown eyes changed to a lighter tone. She grabbed my hand and said, "Follow me."

We left Nebo in the kitchen and Ma and I turned our steps toward the hut. I welcomed the opportunity to face my father, but my struggling heart could not be still. I took in my breath as we approached his bedroom door and held it in to gather every ounce of courage left in me.

"Yassah, is that you?" Father called as soon as we reached his bedroom door.

My heart throbbed louder, beating faster, hammering away. I remained standing behind Ma.

"Someone has come to see you," Ma said, standing in the doorway.

"Who is it?"

"Quonah," she said and stepped aside.

I looked at my Father and my heart inflated with pity, seeing the scrawny body of an old man lying in a fetal position, propping his nappy-haired cheek with a pair of bony hands. Sickness had beaten him like a punishment. His voice was that of my father, but this old man looked nothing like him. Father was a bulldog of a man, handsome and clean-shaved. He fought hard to lift his head, and then managed to turn toward me. I forced a smile to soften my stare. Father made sure his dimmed eyes caught mine, and then he rolled his eye and shut them.

"I do not want to see anyone right now," Father's voice quavered.

He threw me into a state of torment. I felt as though my spirit had been flogged with the whip of madness. I quickly turned to leave.

"Wait...Quonah...please," Ma held me back.

"He will not see me," I said and pulled away.

"Wait here," she insisted.

She left me, walked to Father's bed and knelt beside it.

"Ah...Weaju, your son has come home to see you. Why won't you see him?" she whispered. "No matter what happened in the past, Quonah he is your son...your firstborn...your flesh and blood."

"Yassah, you've never listened to me," Father said in his weak voice. "You never do what I ask. Send the boy away. If Nebo wants to see his dying father, then let him come in. Nebo is the son I know."

Father's voice was neither loud nor tough; it was clear. His dislike for me had not changed. I could not understand his reluctance to abolish our quarrels or make peace with me. Father had refused to reach beyond his pride as I had expected.

Ma stood up, slowly. "You *have* another son!" she snarled. Then, she looked toward the door and caught me as I had turned to leave. She ran toward the door. "Quonah...come back. Give him another chance," she begged as she ran behind my heels.

I stopped. "Can't you see that he resents me?" I shouted. Then trying to control my anger, with great effort, I lowered my voice and tensely said, "Father is not willing to bury the past. Why should I? Why can't you see that? Let him die with his heart closed, I do not care."

"Quonah, [2]I hold your foot," Ma pleaded, lowering her body and touching my feet. "Show your father that a man who shows love is

---

2 *To ask for forgiveness or a favor in the most humble way, one lowers his body and touched the feet of the person whom he is begging.*

not a fainthearted man. The two of you cannot stay angry the same time. One has to give!"

Then Ma lifted her wet face at me, and I saw sorrow and love mingled in her eyes. Her pain demanded my pity and I felt my heart shattered into a thousand pieces. Other than the day I left Mambo Village, I had never seen my mother in such suffering. I reached for her arms and pulled her to stand.

"It is not your fault, Ma," I said, as sympathetically as I could. "Father chooses not to see me. You know how he is...strong-minded. You are not to be blamed. Even if I went back to his room and held his feet, it would not matter. Father will not change his mind. It has already been showed...my father disowns me. As far as he is concerned, I am no longer a part of him."

The doleful expression on her face told me that was not what she had wanted to hear. I thought to convince her otherwise.

"Ma, it does not matter anyway," I said. "I had planned to leave in the evening, but rather than wait until the evening, I will take the next taxi back to the city. I hope Kamara has not left. If he has, I will take any taxi that is available."

Clearly, that was not what Ma had wanted to hear.

"Quonah, you cannot leave just yet," she said quickly. "You just got here."

"It would be better, Ma. Don't you think?"

"Better for whom; you or Weaju? How long has it been since you two had this misunderstanding? Must I be the one to suffer?"

"No, Ma," I said, "I do not want you to suffer."

"Then, why are you not willing to spend more time here? Quonah, I appreciate the things that you send me from the city, but I do not want things. I want to see my son from time to time. I have missed you. I was hoping that you might spend the night with us... after all these years. Is that too much to ask?"

"Ma...."

"Quonah, I have even prepared your favorite dish, fufu with palm-butter. See, I still remember what you like."

"Yeah, Ma, you remembered," I said and chuckled. "Fufu and palm-butter...ah, I've missed it."

"If you do not want to spend the night, just stay awhile and eat what I've prepared for you. After you have eaten, if you still want to leave, I will not hold you back. Okay?"

I smiled at her compromise.

"Have you not missed my cooking?" She asked.

"Oh, Ma, I have. Do you remember how I used to sit in the kitchen...waiting for you to finish cooking?"

"How can I forget? No matter how many times Barchue called you; you would not leave my kitchen. You would wait until I was finished cooking, dished out your food...and then when you've eaten half of it...."

"I would call Barchue," I finished, while laughing. "And, we'd both eat the other half. It was only when you cooked palm-butter. Even on those days when you did not cook fufu for the family, you'd still prepare it just for me. While everybody else was eating rice, you made sure I had fufu. Ma, you cared that I did not go hungry because I did not like rice. Thank you, Ma."

"I love my children, Quonah. I would do anything for you and Nebo. Cooking a favorite dish is the least that I can do."

"Obikai tries to cook it, but nobody cooks palm-butter like you, Ma. Whenever Obikai cooks it, I think about home. And then, I think about Barchue."

"Yes, Barchue," Ma said and forced a smile.

"I will wait and eat what you've prepared Ma...then I will go back to the city."

"Good, that will make me happy. The food will be ready soon, why not go for a walk and think things over. Things have not changed since you left, look around, you'll see. Go," Ma said and motioned for me to leave.

Ma went back to her kitchen and I thought of a place of solitude to clear my head, Small Mountain came to mind. Located two miles outside our village, this huge *bug-a-bug* mount, opposite the creek, had been untouched for unknown reasons. The old people in the village said the mount was there before they were, but no one had used its mud for hut building although it had no sacred value as far as anyone could tell. It was where my best friend, Barchue, and I sat many times sharing secrets.

I thought about Barchue and the senseless troubles we got ourselves into; like hiding the other boys' clothes while they bathed in the creek. A smirk flashed across my face, remembering a great deal more. Whenever Barchue was with me, all my ordeals seemed manageable. His memories made my heart to ache harder, as I was still tending my grief over losing him six months ago in a car accident. I directed my steps and followed the smooth path, made by human-foot traffic, to Small Mountain.

The chirping birds kept me company. Looking at the partially eaten mangos scattered on the ground by the roadside, which had been eaten by wild bats, reminded me of how much I'd missed the beautiful [3]interior. I found myself caught up in a daydream, hearing the wind whistling through the trees. Many times Barchue and I hiked the two-mile trip to his father's sugarcane farm to cut cane for his great-grandmother. We believed the whistling wind to be the ghosts of dead animals, which forced us to run most of the way. And, Barchue's great-grandmother always rewarded us with [4]*country bread.*

As I got closer to Small Mountain, I saw a man sitting at the top with his back toward the path that snaked from the other side of the creek. He took on a strong likeness of Nebo as I got closer.

"Nebo," I called to make sure of it.

He turned around to see his caller. It was Nebo, so I hurried my steps.

"What are you doing here?" Nebo asked as soon as I reached him. Then he made room for me beside him.

"Barchue and I came here daily," I said, as I took my seat beside him. "We used to spy on the girls while they bathed in the creek."

I expected him to laugh or chuckle, but Nebo was not amused by our boyish prank. His face had no sign of either sad or mad emotion.

"Are you okay?" I asked.

He responded with a casual nod. I made no issue of it although I noticed a sudden change in his attitude since I showed Obikai's picture.

"Did Father ever talk to you about Obikai?" I probed further.

Nebo stared at me; I guessed implying I had the nerve to question his knowledge of the family affairs. I was the wandering son, in a manner of speaking, not him.

---

3 *Countryside*
4 *A snack food created from rice. The rice is cleaned, then soaked, then dried over a low fire and then beaten (pounded) in a mortar, producing tiny grains consistency like dry-cereal. Sugar is added and it's eaten dry.*

"Well, did he?" I asked again, clearly insisting I get an answer.

"How could you, Quonah?" Nebo said, staring me in the eyes.

"How could I...what?"

"Why would you choose love over family loyalty?"

Right then, I wanted to tell Nebo about my true stance for Obikai. But at the same time, it seemed a better idea to deliberately deny him my answer. The bad blood between our father and I, which time and distance had suspended, was now staring me in the face. Now, it seemed bigger than life itself. I did not think it was possible to make Nebo understand it, so I remained quiet.

"Um...?" he pressed harder.

"You will not understand it," I said.

"Try me."

"Love governs everything in life, so you must choose love," I said.

Nebo let out a mocking chuckle.

"Seriously, I will always choose love," I said.

"Quonah, what I see is, love seems more important than family... as far as you are concern."

"It is," I said, sarcastically.

"Then there is no family loyalty in you," Nebo said, coldly. "No family loyalty, whatever."

His remarks provoked me, even to anger.

"What is family loyalty to you?" I snarled. "I've communicated with you and Ma over the years, without any efforts on your part. I have looked at no other woman other than my wife. I provide every means for my son to go to school and for his well-being. Is that not family loyalty?"

Nebo stood up. I stood up. We faced each other as if in a duel.

"You are always thinking only about *you*," Nebo pointed at me. "You threw away your family to replace it with a new one. That is not family loyalty!"

"I did not throw my family away for Obikai! I fell in love with my wife."

"You fell in love with your father's wife!"

My anger rose above my self-control.

"I fell in love with a girl...engaged against her will," I shouted.

Nebo squint-eyed me, and then, he walked away. I followed.

"I did not do it just for me," I shouted at his back, following him.

Nebo stopped and turned around to face me.

"I did it because I was thinking about our future," I said, calmly.

"One without a father or a mother or a brother," he said. "What future is that?"

"No, Nebo," I said. "I was thinking about every other young man in this village and the way this tradition of ours forces us into things we do not want. Is it fair to you or me? Choosing the woman I love did not mean that I had no family loyalty. I've loved my family. I've loved my brother. I've loved Ma. I still love the old man. I've loved Obikai and she has loved me, not Father. I did not want any other girls, no matter how many wives were promised me. Why should I have allowed tradition to force me to abandon my true feelings for Obikai? Should I have done what tradition required of me to satisfy them? What about me? What about the other girls I was to marry for the sake of traditions? Oh, Nebo, why should one man want so many wives anyway, when his heart will honor only one? To whom will his heart belong? Where is *his* loyalty?"

Nebo shook his head, as if forcing the message away.

"Father was right," he muttered, "you are a feeble man."

"Father calls me 'feeble' because I refused to follow tradition," I rebutted. "It does not make me a lesser man. Soon you will become a full-fledged man...ready to get a family of your own. How are you going to manage? Is Father going to choose for you a wife?"

Nebo frowned.

"You know nothing about love, Nebo," I said. "Love is a crazy thing, believe me."

There was no need to get worked up. Nebo [5]sucked his teeth and walked away. I chased him down.

"Wait!" I shouted at him.

He ended his march abruptly and our bodies nearly collided.

"Answer me this...do you hate me?" I asked.

Nebo did not make a sound. I reached to touch his shoulder; he pulled away.

"Please Nebo, do not hate me," I pleaded.

He looked away as I was pleading.

Out of frustration, I left Nebo and walked back to the top of Small Mountain and sat down. He looked at me for a minute or so,

---

5 *To hiss a fricative sound uttered as an expression of dislike or contempt*

and then took off with swinging arms and marching steps. I watched Nebo until his image disappeared.

My affection for Obikai was not because of her dancing skills or stunning attraction, although her beauty went beyond simple looks. Obikai and I had deep heartfelt love for each other. Our courtship started when she turned twelve and I was fourteen. It happened five days before she left Mamba Village for her studies at the [6]*Gregree-bush*, the traditional school where young girls transitions into womanhood. While there, girls are lectured on matters of practical importance, indoctrinated with skills of caregiving in their role as mother and wife. The usual time spent in the school is five years, but Obikai stayed for six to advance her dancing. I was eager for her return, more than anyone in Mamba Village was, to the point where I dreamed about her every night during the entire sixth year.

The day finally arrived for her return. All the graduates were robed in short [7]*raffia* skirts, just passed their buttocks. Their bodies and faces were artfully rubbed with white clay; with each graduate showing her own unique design. Obikai wore the gold necklace I had secretly sent her, which hung down slightly above her youthful breasts. On her arms were several gold and silver bangles her father had rewarded her with for her accomplishments. Sporting their school symbol, were ten rows of tiny red and yellow beads; tastefully arranged around her little waist. They fashioned her flat stomach pleasantly. Of all the young women, Obikai had that rare African beauty that is only given to fairytale princesses.

Ten drummers solo the girls with strong passionate beats that built up from a slow swell and grew into steady powerful thumps. The beats subsided into contented weariness and paused. Eight women came out shaking their *sasa* and singing. Then, all twenty young women paraded out stylishly, including Obikai, making their appearance before the mixed audience of family and friends. The girls presented themselves in a semicircle row facing us.

Before their group-dance, each girl danced alone. The excitement in following their feet, dancing and managing rhythm in astonishing ways, was worth the wait. Different body parts moved to

---

6 *Compulsory tribal institutions for men (Poro) and women (Sande) that is responsible to educate the youth for full participation in society. They are conducted in extreme secrecy and are off-limit to non-initiates.*
7 *Skirt made of fiber from dried palm tree leaves woven into material.*

different rhythms of the many drums that were playing. As though the dancer's feet heard one drum, her hips another, her arms and clapping hands, a third drum, her neck and head, a fourth. The girls danced in such a way the audience felt the magic in their legs.

Obikai danced better than all the young women did. The exhilarating movements of her quick feet impressively kept up with the rumbling drums. They moved as though the drum thuds were but an echo of the pounding of her heart reaching out to mine. She finished her dance by slowly extending her palms to the sky, as if in prayer. Her eyes caught mine, and she shyly placed her arms across her chest and covered her breasts. Obikai gleamed like the starlit heavens and joy found its way to my heart.

It took me beyond all reasoning. I felt as if my body had been set on fire and I beamed like an impatient morning sun, burning with desire for her. Whatever I had felt for her had now grown from a childlike passion into a man's natural appetite. She could not escape my eyes. I became blind to everything around me. Obikai became the only woman with whom I wanted to spend the rest of my days.

Fortunately for me, Obikai had returned a freethinking woman. Regardless of what had been taught at the school, stressing the fate of women and the ways in which to please their men, she refused her father's arrangements in becoming my father's bride. I, too, boldly defied my father and married Obikai, against our families' wishes. My father's pride forced him to expel us from his compound. And, because of our defiance, Obikai and I were not allowed to attend functions in the village. She was no longer allowed to dance and that nearly killed her. After all, it is unthinkable to restrict an African from dancing when dancing is in their blood. Finally, the bitterness of our families toward us forced us to move to Palm Trees City, a flourishing town seventy miles from Mambo Village.

I sat on Small Mountain longer than planned, trying to let go of my revived anger. Then, I considered Father's illness and decided to do what my mother had asked me to do, put pride aside. I decided on begging Father for forgiveness and thought to make him understand I did not marry Obikai because of any hatred toward him. So I gathered my courage, got up and hurried back to the village.

As I came in hearing distance, the village echoed with the sound of weeping. Seeing from a great distance, a crowd of people was stationed at our hut. To put my mind at ease, I hurried my steps there, and then to the kitchen, assuming Ma was there. Forcing my way through the crowd, brushing by familiar and unfamiliar faces, I found Ma sitting with Nebo by her side. When she saw me, she faintly stretched out her hand to grab mine.

"Quonah, your father has died," she said, and began crying.

My heart stopped. My knees buckled. Every sound around me fell away. I stood frozen with fear and regret. Then my heart began pounding again. I looked at Nebo; he caught my stare and hung his head.

"Nebo," I called for his attention.

"Yes," he muttered, but refused to lift his head.

"You knew where I was, why did you not come to get me?"

Before Nebo made his answer, Ma said to me, "Quonah, go with the elders, they are taking your father's body to the priest."

I looked toward my parent's hut, indeed, six elders, three men on each side, were marching out of the hut with Father's body on their shoulders.

"Ma, let Nebo go," I said to her.

"We both should go," Nebo suggested and got up.

Nebo and I hurriedly joined the men to escort Father's body to Oldman Jusu's hut.

The ninety-something-year-old priest lived five miles from the edge of Mamba Village, where the deep forest starts. He had the authority to perform all religious rites and administer herbal medicine. Oldman Jusu met us halfway from his front door and directed us to the small shed, about five hundred yards from his hut, where the men laid Father's body.

I remained standing over the body after the men left, wrestling with my sense of right and wrong. Even pride could not steal my grief. Tears ran down my face as I mourned my father's passing. I had not realized how much time had passed until Nebo alerted me.

"Quonah, we are leaving," he shouted.

Nebo had already joined the procession back to the village, so I hurried to catch up. We quietly walked back to the village hearing just the stomps of our marching feet. As we reached the village, the sound of weeping mourners, mixed with singing, aroused my painful regret. Nebo and I went searching for Ma and found her in front of the hut. She stretched her arms out and drew Nebo and I between her shoulders and the three of us wept. Nebo hung his head to hide his tears. I wept openly.

As soon as Ma let go of us, I left she and Nebo and went into the hut, alone. I walked to Father's empty hammock in the sitting area that was tied between the two main sticks holding the roof base. As I was standing there, an intense suffering swallowed me. I did not know whether to laugh or cry. Father never spared the [8]*rattan* for my defiance of lying in his hammock with palm oil stained hands or using it as a swing. I checked my hands and touched the forbidden hammock.

"Quonah," the calm voice of a man startled me.

I withdrew my hand from the hammock quickly, as if I had been caught by its owner.

"Kamara is leaving in twenty minutes," Nebo informed me. "I've asked him to save you the front seat."

I looked at Nebo and forced a smile. Then, I walked to where he was standing, lowered my body, and touched his feet.

"There's no need for that," Nebo said and pulled me up to stand. "You do not have to ask of me, any forgiveness and Father forgave you," he said.

It was something I wanted to hear most. I frowned, showing my skepticism.

"He forgave you," Nebo repeated, as he had read my mind correctly. "When I left you at Small Mountain, I went to see Father because I wanted to hear his side of the story."

"What did he tell you?"

"He said that he did not want to die with a closed heart. Then he said that he was happy to see you, but his pride had made him to send you away. Quonah, it is hard on a man when his own flesh and blood...his son...turns on him. That is how he saw it. Anyhow, he told me to make sure that you knew of his forgiveness. He would have died a longtime ago, but I think he was waiting to see you."

"Nebo, are you sure?"

"Yes," Nebo said, nodding his head. "Here," he handed me the photograph. "I even showed him the picture Ma did not want him to see."

---

8 *Switch made of a long slender stem from palm tree; used for spanking naughty children as a means of discipline.*

"What?"

"It wasn't Obikai that got his attention," Nebo said. "He asked about the boy. Father said the boy looks just like you. He asked me to get Ma, and when we got back to his room, he had died...holding the picture against his heart."

I felt doubtful, but I chose to believe Nebo.

"What about you," I asked Nebo. "Are you angry with me for leaving or are you angry about me not coming back? Which is it? I do not want you to hate me like Father did."

"I do not hate you, Quonah, you are my brother. I was angry with you for not coming back...I missed my big brother. You were not here to teach me how to climb the palm trees, chase opossums, catch birds...like my friends' big brothers taught them. Quonah, the old people say, [9]"When brothers fight to the death, strangers reap their harvest'. What happened between Father and you will never happen to us. There can be no bad blood between us, you are my brother."

Nebo held out his hand, I hugged him instead.

I released him quickly, only to start an unplanned race, which Nebo read correctly. We both took off, squeezing through the front door, and then racing to the kitchen where Ma was. I reached her first, knowing Nebo had deliberately allowed me to beat him.

"Mama, I am sorry," I said, trying to catch my breath. "I swear, I was coming back to patch things up with Father. I knew I could not make-up for time, but I had decided to beg him...I came too late."

"Your father would have forgiven you," Ma replied, not knowing about the conversation Nebo had with Father before he died.

By now, Kamara was urging the passengers to board Little Lamb. Soon all the seats on the bus were occupied, except the front seat which had been kept for me. Kamara sounded his horn for me, long and loud, as if an incredible weight had been placed on the middle of the steering wheel, warning me of wasting his time.

"He is waiting for you," Nebo warned.

"I will be back in two days or so," I said to Ma, while leaving her to board the bus, not in so much of a hurry.

"Go, Quonah, go...they are waiting for you," Ma urged me.

"Ma, do not worry about anything," I said, finally reaching the bus.

---

9 *African parable*

Kamara gave me a pleading stare and I boarded.

As soon as I slammed the door, Little Lamb slow tracked away, burdened with valises, overstuffed bundles, boxes, cages of live chickens, and passengers. I extended my arm out the window and waved until we drove beyond the point where I could no longer see any of the waving relatives.

Saddened by Father's death, I still felt comfort in knowing I could return to Mambo Village without a heavy heart. Better yet, Obikai and little Weaju will come along.

THE BACK OF ONE DOOR
IS
THE FACE OF ANOTHER
—African parable (never give up)—

COMMON THREAD

Known for her animated spirits, Aketi (*a-k-tee*) gloomily walked about during the last two days before the big wedding. She had even abandoned her hefty appetite, and although Sianeh saw that Aketi's humor did not improve, she did not hesitate showing her readiness for the girl's wedding. Sianeh refused to see that Aketi had plunged into the depths of depression, being happy to have found her daughter a good husband, a mature man with many material things to offer her. She considered it lucky that her future son-in-law, Tokpah (*toe-kpa*) Woe, was a successful merchant who lavished his in-laws with gifts. He presented them things that were dear, especially the ones bought in the city shops. For those reasons, Sianeh believed he would care for Aketi well.

Tokpah Woe bought Sianeh a wristwatch although she could not read it. What seemed useless to Sianeh, she adored most. They were simply a *show off* to her friends. When she mentioned to Tokpah Woe that she had no safe place to keep money, he bought her a black handbag. She almost worshipped this bag because of the hidden pocket inside it. It was where she securely zipped her money from would-be thieves. All these things influenced her approval for the marriage.

In spite of everything, there would be no marriage without the father's approval, so Tokpah Woe also bought Aketi's father expensive gifts. He bought two new cutlasses to replace the worn-out ones Nikpa (*ne-pa*) deliberately placed at his feet on the day of the *dowry* negotiation. He also bought a bag of kola nuts, a crate of imported tobacco, and a new pipe. Of all those things, Nikpa's favorite gift was the odd-looking flashlight Tokpah Woe presented him last. Nikpa made the remark, 'who can buy battery for such an odd looking flashlight?' and Tokpah Woe showed him the odd battery that went with the flashlight. Nikpa laughed hysterically, knowing when his friends see it they would envy him for such possessions. Although Tokpah Woe had no rank in his town, Nikpa and Sianeh thought highly of their future son-in-law because of their gifts.

The same day Tokpah Woe brought the gifts, he paid the dowry at the end of his visit. Like a big shot, he pulled out a bundle of money from his pocket, counted two hundred and fifty dollars to pay. Sianeh's eager eyes guarded the suitor's hand while he handed the money to Nikpa.

"Here is two hundred and fifty dollars...you may count it if you like," Tokpah Woe said to Nikpa. "This is the dowry you have requested."

"I do not need to count it," Nikpa said. "Tokpah Woe, you are a ¹*big* man, if you say there is two hundred and fifty dollars here, I believe you."

Nikpa stuffed the folded bills in his pocket, which he counted as soon as Tokpah Woe left the compound.

Tokpah Woe counted an extra twenty-five dollars and handed the money to Sianeh, which she grabbed, smiling from ear to ear, and shoved it down her bosom.

"I will put it in my hiding place later," Sianeh said, jokingly. "When they say 'luck comes to only special people', they are talking about my daughter. See, Aketi is a lucky girl to have gotten a *real* man like you, Tokpah Woe. I've always known you would be a good man for my daughter."

Tokpah Woe smiled to Sianeh's praise and extended his hand to Nikpa to close the deal.

"Some people say love and affection have no place in a dowry transaction, still I have planned good things for the girl," he said to Nikpa. "I've prepared to make your daughter my ²*head wife* although she is my fifth. Nikpa, God is my witness...I've never paid that much for a wife," he finished with an annoying boyish grin.

"Mind my daughter," Nikpa said, as they shook hands and snapped fingers.

Nikpa chuckled to his future son-in-law's arrogant behavior,

1 *A man worthy of respect*
2 *The first wife the man marries; she remains his head wife during his & her lifetime. She is responsible for any subsequent wives he marries, and it is with her that he consults concerning matters involving the family. However, it is possible for a man to bestow that position on a subsequent wife even if he is still married to the original head wife.*

partly out of envy. Neither he nor any other man in his family had paid that much for a bride-price. Nikpa was able to pay only fifty dollars, in four installments, to each of his father-in-law.

The arrangement for the marriage took place without Aketi's knowledge or consent, mainly because children do not concern themselves with their parents' guests. The only time Aketi met Tokpah Woe was on the day before she left home to attend the *Gregree-bush* school. Eleven-year-old Aketi was called to Nikpa's hut so Tokpah Woe could see her. As he approached the girl, to present the gold necklace he brought her, Aketi shyly covered her underdeveloped breasts to protect them from the slightest meeting of his eager hands. The instant he placed the gift around her neck, Aketi responded with a childish giggle. Then she ran to rejoin her sisters, Kaela (*k-lor*) and Teta, to resume their girlish activities. At the end of the day, the necklace ended in Sianeh's hand, cautioning Aketi that she might lose it.

Two days after Aketi returned home from the *Gregree-bush,* as the wedding had been prearranged, Tokpah Woe came to claim his bride. Heavy rain had prevented the [3]*kitchen party* that Sianeh had planned for her daughter on the day before, so she suggested to the women that Aketi's gifts be given at the wedding.

On the eve of the wedding, Aketi remained awake throughout the drizzling night while the others were deep in sleep. It was neither the falling rain, nor the pleasing noise of the wind teasing the *thatch* roof that kept her from sleeping. The upside-down thrill of her childhood ending days had crept into reality. The wedding day had arrived and she was not ready to become any man's wife. Awake and absorbed in her thoughts, Aketi imagined the time she and her sisters sat gossiping about Nikpa's friends, making fun of them and giving names according to their appearances.

"Zeeka looks like a crocodile that walks like a man," Teta joked, mocking the man's wobbling steps.

"And Nowa, his wife, resembles a doe," Aketi added.

The girls laughed hysterically.

Nowa was nearly five-feet-nine-inches tall, with a slender body. She and her husband never walked side by side because Zeeka stood only five-feet-two inches high and weighed close to two hundred fifty pounds.

---

3 *A party of women relatives and friends assembled to present gifts (usually of a specified kind for household use) for the bride.*

Another evening while the girls sat around the [4]*fire* in Sianeh's kitchen, Teta noticed some [5]*pawpaws,* resembling breasts of different shapes, while they hung from the tops of their lengthened trunks.

"For sure, one day ours will look like that," Teta joked, pointing at the pawpaws.

Aketi and Kaela laughed at the sighting, seeing the close resemblance of the pawpaws to a woman's breast. Being Nikpa's head wife, Sianeh felt it was her duty to discipline his daughters. She wasted no time in scolding the girls.

"I have warned you, time and again, behaving childishly will prevent you from attracting a good man," Sianeh quarreled.

The girls' laughter quickly changed to giggles before dying out.

The more Aketi thought about leaving her sisters, the more sadness occupied her heart, the more she hated the wedding. The three girls were close although they each had a different mother and three years separated their ages. Their willingness to help one another with chores bound Aketi, Kaela, and Teta like three peas in a pod. None of their mothers had to intervene in any of their conflicts. The trio had the reputation to even swap dresses, being nearly the same size.

Nikpa had married three women. Sianeh, his first wife, had three children with him after losing the first four in childbirth; Aketi and her two brothers, Yoma and Clay. He had always shown Sianeh partiality because she had given him boy children, and did not care to spare the feelings of his other wives. His second wife, Dahoe, had four children; Teta and three other daughters. Bendu, Nikpa's third wife, delivered for him four daughters, including Kaela. Bendu was expecting her fifth child, which Nikpa suspected to be a girl child because of her repulsive attitude towards him during all her pregnancies. He thought of taking in another wife, but could not afford to and placed the blame on his wives because they had not given him enough sons to take over his farming, knowing their daughters would eventually desert the family to follow their husbands. For those reasons, Nikpa kept just three wives.

Four huts were built in his compound with the help of his [6]*work*

---

4 A three-stoned hearth built for cooking

5 (Papaya) tropical fruit; large, oblong, yellowish-orange like a melon; has many tiny black seeds

6 Communal ritual which the whole village society participates; a group of men gathered to help build a hut or clear land for farming for the owner. During that time, he secures the services of a musician, who drums and sings as the men work. His wives (or women) cook hearty meals for all the workers.

group. Each wife's hut had a small kitchen attached to it, but it was Sianeh's kitchen the family gathered around the fire and told of the day events. Nikpa joined his family only when he felt like it or to hear the quarrels between his wives if there were any. Each wife shared a hut with her children and Nikpa lived alone in the largest hut of his establishment, where he entertained his guests. He visited his wives in their huts on occasions when his in-laws were visiting or a wife would visit his hut at his request. Such was the organization of Nikpa's compound.

Yoma and Clay attended the local public school while the girls helped their mothers with the cooking, cleaning, fishing, or weaving baskets and fishing nets. The boys went to their father's hut each day after school to show him what they had learned and recounted stories to Nikpa based on the pictures in the books. He felt proud that his sons were more knowledgeable than his friends' sons. Based on the information collected from the stories, Nikpa boasted that when the boys become more educated, they would care for him so he does not work too hard. He was looking forward to the promises of Yoma and Clay to buy him a taxi and teach him how to drive it. Yoma promised to westernize their father's hut by replacing his palm *thatch* roof with [7]zinc. While his acquaintances kept their sons working on their farms all-day instead of sending them to school, educating Yoma and Clay would enable them to teach him many things. He was doing for his sons what his father did not do for him.

Although Nikpa was not a rich man, according to Sianeh's standards, he provided for his family as well as any ordinary man. To help with the boys' schooling, she planted a small pepper patch near her hut and made [8]oil to sell so she could donate money for school clothes. Aketi often hinted to Sianeh about attending school, but Sianeh ignored her daughter's wishes. Under the urging of her heart, she would make sure that Aketi marry a well-off man. As for her sons, Sianeh made sure they did not look like some of their friends who wore shirts that did not come together in the front because they had clearly outgrown them. Those friends received a new shirt only during the Christmas holiday. Yoma and Clay were given new shirts at the beginning of each school semester and Christmas. Most par-

7 *Aluminum sheets used for shingles*
8 *Reference to palm (nuts) oil – palm oil is produced by skimming the pounded pulp of the cooked palm nuts.*

ents in the village could not afford more than the [9]bumbors their children wore throughout the year.

After a rainy night in Africa, the first morning ray of light breaks with sparkling freshness and the entire place is wonderfully clean. Everything glitters as if the village is newly made. By midmorning, preparations for the wedding went underway. Every kitchen in Nikpa's compound was full of activities as savory smells from cooking pots covered his yard. Two of Sianeh's sisters, Hawa and Korto, joined her close friends in her kitchen to help with the cooking. The constant banging of the [10]pestle sounded more like music than noise as two women pounded [11]dumbboy in one [12]mortar with perfectly timed rhythm. As one woman pounded the boiled cassava pieces with her pestle, the other woman's pestle was raised. Two other women maneuvered their pestles up and down in another mortar, [13]beating the [14]new rice Korto's husband had sent. Using one of the two [15]fanners she had brought from her house to speed things up, Korto helped by [16]fanning the rice to rid it of husks.

All the young women helped the women in the kitchen by [17]picking rice or washing dishes. Yoma and his friends horsed around while tactically placing fresh-cut palm branches around the compound. Clay hurriedly swept the yard with the [18]twig-broom Nikpa handed him with keen instructions, when the boy was finished, not one piece of leaf was to be found on the ground. Nikpa wanted every bit of the earth swept well. The tracks from the palm broom were to be visible, especially in front of his hut. His guest spying any litter on the ground of his compound is a disgrace to him. To Clay's delight, there was no need to sprinkle water on the earth to settle the dust because last night's rain had done it for him.

---

9 A single strip of cloth that is wrapped around the waist and then between the legs; it is sometimes worn as the sole object of clothing, especially by young boys.
10 A long wooden pole
11 Boiled cassava pounded into a thick sticky dough
12 A wooden receptacle fashioned from a hollowed-out tree trunk. Food substance is placed in it to beat.
13 Working in rhythm, the pestle is thrust to the bottom of the mortar in an almost dance-like steady beat to begin the process of food preparation.
14 Fresh-cut dried rice still covered with husks
15 A flat basket used to winnow rice by blowing away the chaff grains
16 Tossing the rice grains in a fanner to rid it of chaffs
17 To remove those rice grains that did not shell out of their pods during the beating process.
18 The central palm branch or the veins of the palm branch are bunched together and tied; the tips makes a high-quality broom

Early that morning Tokpah Woe hired a driver to take more things to Nikpa's compound for the celebration. Sianeh gladly accepted the things, but with some criticism. The twenty-one white hens were good size, however she complained about the two goats and the cow being small. The driver had no listening ears. While they unloaded the things out of the Toyota pickup, he mumbled to his helper that it was impossible to satisfy a woman. The driver also told Nikpa that all fifteen cases of [19]*Club Beer* and twenty-four crates of soft drinks were for the celebration; however, the entire case of Schnapps belonged to Nikpa. Tokpah Woe wanted to make him happy on his daughter's wedding day.

Close to midmorning, Aketi finally decided to confront her mother about the wedding. She reluctantly left her room and went to Sianeh's kitchen. When Sianeh saw her daughter coming, she put down the food she was tending and welcomed Aketi in the kitchen with a joke.

"Save your energy for your new husband tonight," Sianeh teased, thinking Aketi had come to lend a hand.

The women exploded into boisterous laughter. Some of them even expressed envy for the young bride, recounting the morning of their own wedding. Aketi stopped, turned and hurried her steps back to her room.

"She has not spoken a word since I arrived here yesterday," Korto said to Sianeh. "Has she talked to you about the marriage?"

Before Sianeh could make an answer, one of the women pointed at a middle-aged man approaching the kitchen with a package.

"Is that Tokpah Woe who is coming?" the woman asked.

"Yes, it is Tokpah Woe," Sianeh answered and quickly abandoned the pan of chopped chicken she was tending. She ran to meet him and then led him to her hut.

"Is the woman happy?" Tokpah Woe asked Sianeh, being concerned that news had reached him suggesting the bride's discontent of the marriage. The driver had also mentioned that Sianeh was not satisfied about the cow, but Tokpah Woe did not care to feed Sianeh's [20]*long eye*. He did not mention it to her.

"She is happy," Sianeh assured him. "It is her wedding, why shouldn't she be happy?"

19 *Main brand commercial brewed beer in Liberia*
20 *Liberian slang for an expression of greed*

"Someone told the driver the woman was not happy."

"Tokpah Woe, do not worry," Sianeh stressed. "Some people say things out of envy. My daughter has a good man. Besides, have you forgotten? You do not remember anything on this day because men are always too drunk to remember their wedding day. Only the woman remembers. The woman thinks about the marriage and about leaving her mother's home which fills her heart with some sadness, but it is not much to build a concern. Aketi is only thinking about those things she will miss. I went through it, myself; so did my sisters and my friends. All changes after the wedding, especially when her husband starts to make her happy. Promise me Tokpah Woe, that you will make my daughter happy. Now tell me, what is in the package?"

Tokpah Woe accepted Sianeh's explanation for what it was worth.

"A new dress for Aketi," he said happily. It was not made by any of our local tailors. I went to Palm Trees City and bought it from the white man store."

His bragging pleased Sianeh; she playfully hit his shoulders and chuckled.

"In fact, there are two dresses in here," Tokpah Woe added. "The red dress is for you," he handed the package to Sianeh.

She wiped her hands on her lappa to clean it of fresh chicken odor and grabbed the package.

"Was mine also bought from the white man's store?"

Tokpah Woe looked at Sianeh. "Yes," he said and chuckled.

"People tell me Aketi is lucky," Sianeh went on. "It is mainly because you are a generous man. Some of the women have openly wished for a son-in-law like you. Who wouldn't want a man like you?"

Tokpah Woe busted out laughing as Sianeh's words had put his mind to rest. Because of all the gifts he had offered, it was good for his [21]heart to sit down.

"Go to Nikpa's place," Sianeh suggested. "The men are there waiting for you. It is bad luck to see the bride before the ceremony."

Aketi's ears had caught their whispers from the doorway, she straightened her dress and sat up on her bed to receive them, thinking Tokpah Woe will enter the room also. Instead, Tokpah Woe

---

21 *Liberian slang indicating freedom from or ease of worrying*

walked off and headed to Nikpa's hut. Sianeh entered the room with a bright smile.

"Your husband has brought you a new dress," Sianeh announced with excitement and dropped the package on the bed.

To Sianeh's dismay, Aketi slowly turned her face away.

"Open the package so we can see what the dresses look like," Sianeh suggested still. "They were bought from the white man store, you know. The red dress is mine. Isn't Tokpah Woe a good man? Go ahead...open it."

"Mama," Aketi mumbled, but did not look at her mother.

"Yes, my daughter, what is it? Look at me."

Aketi slowly turned her face and Sianeh saw the tearstains, detecting trouble. Sianeh drew in a long, deep breath and slumped on the bed next to her daughter.

"They say when it rains on the day of your wedding, you cry during your entire marriage. Is that why you are crying?" Sianeh asked, concerned.

Aketi made no answer.

"It is not so," Sianeh said. "It rained the entire day of my wedding, but have you seen me cry in your father's compound?"

Aketi made no answer.

"I have never shed a tear since Nikpa brought me here," Sianeh went on. "Aketi, please listen to me. You should be happy because today is your wedding. You're lucky that Tokpah Woe is a generous man. My husband is a good man, but a man like Tokpah Woe would have made a better provider. I would not have had to work so hard to help with your brothers' schooling. Tokpah Woe has enough money to take care of his wives and his in-laws. Most men are not able to do that. Can't you see it?"

"Mama, I want to say something," Aketi pleaded, as respectfully as she could, knowing Sianeh's reaction would be unacceptable.

"Is it about the marriage?"

"No," Aketi said.

Sianeh smiled and asked, "What is it?"

"Mama, why do you not treat me like you do Yoma and Clay?"

As the words sank in, Sianeh made a grunting sound. "What do you mean?" she then asked. "I treat all my children fairly, even those by the other women. I've worked hard to send my sons to school. As for my daughter, I have found a man that can take good care of her. What have I done for your brothers that I have not done for you?"

"I want to go to school," Aketi mumbled.

Sianeh frowned. She could not believe Aketi had the nerve to show ingratitude when she had found her a good man. Judging from the girl's behavior, she concluded her daughter did not want the marriage. Sianeh tugged away her patience and allowed anger to take over her face.

"Never compare a girl to her brothers," Sianeh scolded. "A woman cannot compare herself to a man. Have you ever seen it or heard of it? One day your brothers will become respectable men. Aketi, you will remain a mere woman. It is better you accept your role as fate has chosen it for you. I did not choose it for you. Neither did I choose it for me. I accepted my fate because it is what God has given me. It was chosen for our mothers as well, so you should do the same, Aketi."

Tears filled Aketi's eyes. As it dribbled down her face, this enraged Sianeh further.

"Look at your face!" she shouted. "Why should you portray a woman of sorrow on the day you should be happy? Why are you painting your face with grief as if someone has died? Have I not given you all a mother can give? I have done far better than most mothers in this village have. None of my friends have found a better husband for their daughters as I have. I have laid down my neck for you, still you are not satisfied. Is this my reward? What am I to do with you, Aketi?"

"I do not want to marry Tokpah Woe either," Aketi moaned.

"What do you mean by that? Are you not going to marry the man I have found for you?" Sianeh shouted.

Aketi made no answer.

"In fact, you have no saying in the matter," Sianeh said, shrugging her shoulders.

"Mama, I want to go to school with Yoma and Clay," Aketi said, sobbing.

Sianeh's face twisted with an overwhelming rush of anger. She jumped off the bed, dashed out of the room, and headed for the kitchen. Sianeh staggered out the front door and intentionally threw her body to the ground, making sure the women in the kitchen saw her laying flat on her back.

"Sianeh has fainted!" Hawa alerted the women and ran out of the kitchen to her sister.

The rest of the women rushed out of the kitchen to where Sianeh was lying and formed a circle around her. With the help of two other women, Hawa and Korto struggled to lift their sister and then carried her to her room. Korto ordered Yoma to tell Nikpa what had happened so he comes to his wife's aid. However, Nikpa did not come to Sianeh's hut. Instead, he yelled at the boy, telling him that it is expected that Sianeh grieve on the day her daughter was marrying. Nikpa added that Sianeh's sisters had come for such a purpose and a man could do nothing about it. He remained in his hut and resumed drinking *palm-wine* with Tokpah Woe and the other men, as they were laughing at negative women-jokes made by Vokai (*vo-kai*), his eighty-year-old uncle.

The women crowded Sianeh's room, debating with each other the reason she had fainted. Some of the women suggested Sianeh was overwhelmed with joy. Others argued she was clearly stricken with grief because her daughter was leaving home for good. Hawa tore off a piece of cardboard from the big box that Sianeh had saved to collect the gifts from Aketi's kitchen party and began fanning the air over her inconsolable sister. Korto began wiping Sianeh's forehead with a dampened rag, which one woman thoughtfully handed her, to provide more comfort.

Sianeh came to herself, mumbling and moaning, "Ah, my people, my [22]heart is hurting."

"What's the matter?" Hawa asked.

"My daughter has gone mad," Sianeh cried, "Aketi is pushing me into humiliation."

"What do you mean, Sianeh?" Korto asked. "Why are you grieving like a widow?"

"You would not believe it, but Aketi is refusing the marriage," Sianeh said, sobbing. "She wants to kill me today...I cannot believe it. Do you think that a son would have done this thing to his mother? It was good that God took my other daughters before Aketi. Who can go through this more than once? You are all my witnesses, Aketi wants my friends to celebrate my passing instead of her wedding," Sianeh broke down, weeping with convulsive gasping.

---

22 Liberian slang to express emotional let-down

"Stop, Sianeh...please!" Korto begged. "God did not take your children because of that. Children are our blessings."

"What blessings? This is not a blessing, it is a curse! Aketi has brought shame into my yard. Today, when all my friends are here with me, she has brought shame on my head. How am I to show my face after today? Do you not know that shame kills faster than a disease...Aketi has killed me. She has given me a good dose of shame poison to eat. I am dying, my people, I am dying!"

"Sorry, Mama," Aketi said, sorrowfully. "I do not want to kill you."

"What are you sorry about?" Sianeh shouted at Aketi. "Have you changed your mind about the marriage? Are you going to accept the marriage?"

Aketi stood with downcast eyes. She made no answer.

"Then you're not sorry," Sianeh shouted. "How can you tell me that you're sorry?"

"Mama, why should you pass me to a man that is as old as my father? I am like Yoma and Clay, I'm not a basket...I have a heart."

Seemingly, Aketi's respect for her mother was getting out of hand, so Hawa thought it wise to intervene.

"Do not speak to your mother in that way!" Hawa urged, waving her finger at Aketi's face. "Have you gone crazy?"

Then to save Sianeh's pride, Hawa ordered the women to leave the room. She did not want outsiders witnessing their family problem, which was worthy of ugly rumors. The women reluctantly walked out except Mattus and Zia, they got as far as the door and remained standing. Although Hawa did not live in Sass Town, she knew of the women's history through Sianeh's warning. Their ears tingled upon hearing gossips. Mattus and Zia were [23]*chay-chay polays,* expert at turning flickers of information into misguided flames of gossips.

"You must *all* leave," Hawa strongly urged the women.

Mattus sucked her teeth and walked out. Zia rolled her eyes and followed.

The news reached Nikpa's hut in a short time that Aketi had refused the marriage. Yoma remained standing until all was told. He added that because of Sianeh passing out, he was not sure whether his mother was dead or alive. His aunty Hawa had stopped him from following the women into the bedroom so he did not have the op-

---

23 *Liberian slang for a gossiper or one who carries news*

portunity to know exactly what had happened to her. Nikpa was to hurry to his wife's hut, on his sisters-in-law urging.

The unfavorable news also met Tokpah Woe with drunkenness, but he was not yet beyond reasoning. Tokpah Woe got up with the intention of following Nikpa.

"Wait here," Nikpa said to Tokpah Woe and left his hut hurriedly.

Nikpa could not afford to allow his compound to appear out of control. He hurried to Sianeh's hut, mumbling his plan of how he will handle things.

"Aketi...Aketi!" Nikpa shouted at the top of his lungs.

He reached Sianeh's place, and rushed through the door. Nikpa was eager to put sense into his daughter's head and return to his guests. Sianeh jumped off her bed, dried her face, and began pulling at the wrinkles to fix her lappa. Nikpa rolled his eyes at his wife, blaming her for spoiling his good time with his friends.

"Tell Nikpa what you have done!" Sianeh shouted at Aketi. "Tell him...I cannot speak such news with my mouth."

Aketi looked at Nikpa, but stood mute.

"Are you not going to tell him?" Sianeh went on. "Go ahead and tell him," she shoved Aketi's shoulders.

"I do not want to marry Tokpah Woe," Aketi muttered tearfully.

Fueled with anger, Nikpa stretched his eyes and raised his hand to strike Aketi.

Hawa grabbed Nikpa's hand and held it back. "Nikpa, don't hit her while you are angry," she pleaded.

"What did you say?" Nikpa asked Aketi, keeping his hand high, wanting to be sure of her defiance, and daring her to repeat.

"I do not want to marry Tokpah Woe," Aketi repeated.

Nikpa pulled his hand from Hawa's grip and slapped his daughter's mouth hard, leaving a handprint on her skin. Aketi stood in a daze, feeling pain and disbelief. She covered her mouth as tears rolled down her cheeks. Nikpa stood trembling with fury, clearly, rage had taken control of him. He had never lost control to the point of hitting any of his children.

"Have you gone mad?" Nikpa yelled. "Do you know what happens to a woman who has no husband? Do you want to be a freed-woman who has no respect in her community? Any man can claim her whenever he wants to. Is that the kind of woman, you wish to become?"

Aketi made no answer.

"I will make it clear to you, Aketi," Nikpa said, still trembling. "There is no happiness outside a marriage...not even for a man. Such a life is not good for a woman. As long as there is life in my body, none of my daughters will be like those women. You are going to marry the man your mother has found you...even if it kills you!" Nikpa finished and stormed out of the room.

The effects in his failure to present Tokpah Woe his bride dawned on him. Nikpa took four giant steps and stopped in his tracks, knowing he would not be able to face such humiliation if Aketi openly disobey him. What would his friends say behind his back? Would his other daughters also follow Aketi's footsteps? Aketi had already pushed him into hitting her, which by his standard was the duty of their mothers. The ordeal seemed troubling.

Nikpa had kept a good name up to the time he beat his wife, Bendu, for running away when she first came to his compound. This wife-beating did not spoil Nikpa's name. The women in the village did not like it, but as far as the village elders were concerned, Bendu had provoked Nikpa because of her defiance. Faced with this new ordeal, nothing else would satisfy him other than the marriage.

Nikpa turned around and took his steps back to Sianeh's hut. He found Yoma standing by the door and quickly ordered his son, in a most harsh manner, to call Tokpah Woe. The boy was to make certain that only Tokpah Woe is escorted to Sianeh's hut. Yoma waited until Nikpa's order was completed, nodding at the end of every statement, and then he took off running.

Nikpa gathered his wives and sisters-in-law to a meeting, but refused Oldman Vokai's offer to attend the meeting. There would be no negotiations so he did not need another man other than Tokpah Woe. As soon as Tokpah Woe entered Sianeh's hut, everyone settled in the sitting area and waited for Nikpa to start.

"I am sorry about this thing that has happened," Nikpa began with an apology to Tokpah Woe. "When a man like Tokpah Woe has appealed for acceptance into one's family, he should be given the utmost respect. My daughter wants to behave foolishly, but I will not allow it. These days some of the girls fill their heads with nonsense, but I will not allow any of my daughters to do such. Aketi has become

[24]*frisky*, to the point where she has told her mother she does not want the marriage."

Tokpah Woe frowned at the news, especially when Sianeh had reassured him his bride was ready for the marriage. He wanted to ask about the marriage rejection, but Nikpa stopped him.

"Wait, let me finish," Nikpa advised. "Aketi is young and does not know better. It is left with you to be patient. You are to teach her what is good in having a husband."

Then Nikpa recounted how he experienced trouble with Bendu his wife. He had to teach Bendu that when a woman marries, her voice was to remain silent. It was her husband's voice to obey, not hers for him to obey.

Tokpah Woe extended his hand and accepted Nikpa's right and proper apology. The men shook hands and snapped fingers.

Nikpa turned to Sianeh and said, "This nonsense must stop. The marriage will take place today. Call the women back to your kitchen so you can continue with the preparations." Then he said to Tokpah Woe, "Follow me back to my hut so the women can finish their work. I expect no more trouble out of Aketi."

Aketi stood starring at Tokpah Woe's face. His scarred tribal marks distinguished him among his people and proved him worthy of the utmost respect, but his silvery temples, showing youth in its decline, offended her. Her heart ached in her chest, for the fact she had no understanding of Tokpah Woe's eagerness to steal her youthful body. He reminded her of her father, Nikpa, a wife-beater who only care about his sons. In spite of what Nikpa had said, Aketi decided she would not marry Tokpah Woe regardless of the consequences.

As Nikpa and Tokpah Woe were taking their steps back to Nikpa's hut, Aketi said, not quite inaudibly, "I am not going with Tokpah Woe."

Nikpa stopped. "What did you say?" he asked, thinking he had heard wrong.

"Paapa, I do not want to marry him," Aketi repeated, looking at her suitor.

Nikpa's stare gave the impression of being annoyed beyond measure. He grabbed his long sleeves at the hem and slowly rolled each

---

24 *Liberian slang for being rebellious or disobedient*

sleeve up as far as his elbow, one arm at a time, all the while staring at Aketi. Then he looked at Tokpah Woe, whose face seemed dressed with embarrassment. He could not imagine what Tokpah Woe was thinking. Nikpa's own stomach could not take his daughter's provocation, Aketi had openly shamed him. Nikpa looked at his wives, and then at Aketi.

Not a word was uttered by anyone.

"What have I done to deserve this?" Nikpa said, as if petitioning to his wives for pity. "Why must Aketi disrespect me in the face of strangers? Where is it tolerated the child disciplines the parent? Correct me if I am wrong. None of these women have ever gone against me...Aketi will not be the one to change that. Because she does not want to marry Tokpah Woe, is that the way it is to be? Aketi is a mere woman and she is too stupid to realize it for her own good. Even if it kills her, she is going to marry the man her mother has found for her."

Nikpa's three wives and two sisters-in-law stood listening.

"I have come to claim a wife, not a ghost," Tokpah Woe said jokingly, but with seriousness.

"I promise you, Tokpah Woe, Aketi will leave my compound today as your wife. I have given you my word. She is young and headstrong, perhaps foolish, so never mind what she is saying. Aketi will do what she is told...I am the one who wears the trousers in this compound."

"Can a woman obey her husband when she has openly defied her own father?" Tokpah Woe snarled, frowning.

Nikpa ignored Tokpah Woe for the sake of harmony.

"No, Nikpa, tell me honestly...uh," Tokpah Woe insisted. "Has 'change' come to your compound and not ours? I have not seen this anywhere else. These women here, do they have voices or what? I have not come to disrespect you, Nikpa...."

"Did I not tell you about Bendu?" Nikpa shouted, less tolerant of Tokpah Woe's continuous taunting. "Did I not tell you how she behaved when I first brought her here to my compound? Were you not listening? Is my compound the only place where a woman has tried to provoke her husband?"

"I've heard every word that came out of your mouth," Tokpah Woe replied. "I have already paid a dowry, do you agree or not?"

"I agree."

"Will I leave your compound with my wife?" Tokpah Woe asked.

"Aketi is practically your wife, is she not?"

"Yes, but...."

"Aketi will go with you today," Nikpa shouted. "Those are the words coming out of my mouth! Did you hear them?"

"Nikpa, I hear you, but your daughter must go with me willingly," Tokpah Woe said calmly. "I cannot take a woman who will cause trouble in my home. Will she go freely? Will she, too, run away?"

Sianeh was not sure of butting in. While the men went back and forth, she simply shifted her attention to the talker. Hawa and Korto were mainly there to give Sianeh support, so neither woman thought it wise to get involved. Being Sianeh's oldest sister, Hawa considered it okay to meddle in her sister's affairs, but must do so with caution by first addressing Nikpa. Hawa raised her hand to get Nikpa permission, out of respect for him, and he nodded, recognizing her.

"Nikpa, hear me out," Hawa pleaded. "Allow me to talk to Aketi, maybe she will listen to me."

Nikpa cut his eyes and nodded. To soften his anger, Hawa thought it wise to feed his ego.

"Because of my sister, Sianeh, you have always treated me kindly," Hawa praised Nikpa. "I say it with a clear heart…you are a good man."

Nikpa glanced at Tokpah Woe and forced a smile. Seemingly, Hawa had gotten on his good side.

"I thank God that I am able to witness my sister's daughter enter into marriage," Hawa continued. "This day should be a happy day in Sianeh's life."

"Instead, our sister is weeping," Korto interrupted, [25]pushing up fire.

"Thank you, Korto, thank you…I am happy you've agreed with me," Hawa said. "A marriage ceremony is not a place for mourning. I do not know why Aketi does not understand it. She has foolishly refused to listen to her own mother, maybe she will listen to me. Am I not Sianeh's big sister?"

"Hawa, we are not here for long talks," Nikpa complained.

---

25 *Liberian slang meaning to instigate, provoke or stir up*

"I know Nikpa, but hear me first. Our mother is no longer with us, in that case, does it not make me Sianeh's mother? Is it not so?"

"Yes," Nikpa answered impolitely.

"See, I have every right to say something to you," Hawa said to Aketi.

Aketi made no answer.

"Aketi, you must listen to me," Hawa advised. "The path of life is not smooth for a woman, so you must walk soft in it. Your husband's voice is yours to obey, do it quietly so there is no trouble in your home. When your mother has found you a good man, it is done so things are not difficult for you. No one has testified to any wrong doings on Tokpah Woe's part. He does not beat his wives. Many witnesses from his village have confirmed this. So far, Tokpah Woe has treated you well. He has pleased your father also. What is it that turns your heart away from him?"

Aketi made no answer.

"I know what you are feeling," Hawa continued. "It is not because of Tokpah Woe...it is the marriage. You are afraid of leaving your mother's hut. Is it not so?"

"That is foolishness!" Nikpa shouted.

"Please, Nikpa...let me finish," Hawa pleaded.

"Do it hurriedly, Hawa," Sianeh urged her sister. "Do not let my husband get angry with us too."

"Sianeh, we have each followed our mother's footsteps, so must Aketi," Hawa continued. "She cannot live in your hut for the rest of her life. One day she will leave to set up a home of her own. That day is today."

"That's true," Sianeh agreed.

"Aketi, go with the man your mother has found for you," Hawa said. "First, beg Tokpah Woe his pardon before you leave your mother's hut. He will forgive you. Men always pay attention to the pleading voice of a woman."

Hawa finished and reached for Sianeh's hand. She had dipped into her sister's affairs as far as she could dare; telling Aketi her tradition was to insure her place in life rather than a choice that might lead her astray. A woman's place is a position of simplicity, but she was anything but simple to her husband. The decision to turn her back on this tradition rested with her and nobody else. In any case, Nikpa's promise to Tokpah Woe was to be kept. Aketi was to consider everyone, not just herself.

The room transformed to a more peaceful tone after Hawa's lecture, even Aketi was no longer pouting. Everyone waited on her to beg Tokpah Woe his pardon. Aketi looked at Tokpah Woe and then at Nikpa.

"I am sorry, Paapa," Aketi apologized calmly to Nikpa. "I've not chosen to disobey you, it is true. I beg you, Paapa, forgive me."

Nikpa responded with a grunt.

Then Aketi turned to Hawa, who was holding Sianeh's hand.

"Aunty Hawa, I'm begging you and Aunty Korto to forgive me also. You are my mother's guests, I am grateful for your coming."

"I forgive you, Aketi," Hawa said. "Now, beg your mother for her forgiveness."

Aketi nodded and turned to Sianeh.

"Mama, I am sorry," she said, "I did not mean to cause you any misery. I see that you've done well for me."

Sianeh grunted.

Aketi turned toward Tokpah Woe and paused.

"Aketi, you must continue," Hawa urged.

Aketi looked at Tokpah Woe. She could not say his name as his name seemed stuck in her throat.

"Aketi…finish what you've started," Hawa urged. "Say his name… Tokpah Woe. Say it."

Aketi stood staring.

"Aketi…beg the man so we can go back to cooking the food," Korto urged. "He is waiting on you."

Nikpa grunted, pushing Aketi into continuing.

"What you have done is what any man is expected to do," Aketi said to Tokpah Woe, not addressing him properly, by his name. "With my father's promise, you have considered this marriage with a dowry. Your money and gifts have won the hearts of my family…now our culture is forcing me to accept it. I'm expected to follow a man far more mature than my age. I have no quarrels with you, Tokpah Woe," she said his name finally. "But there's an ugly sadness in my heart. The man I am to spend my life with has not won my own heart."

Nikpa could not believe what he was hearing.

"Aketi, [26]mind your mouth," Nikpa snarled, warning her, that as far as he was concerned, she had already taken her defiance beyond disrespect.

Aketi paused.

"Wait Nikpa, let her finish," Hawa pleaded.

"What is she to finish?" Nikpa asked angrily.

"Nikpa, Please," Hawa pleaded. "Go on Aketi."

Aketi looked at Tokpah Woe.

"This sadness will make you hate me," she said, staring at him, not blinking once. "How could I blame you for it? That future scares me. I do not know anything about [27]man-business, but I know men never see the line between love and a woman's acceptance for reasons of her duties. A woman is forced into an arranged marriage and she is expected to accept it because it is her duty. Tokpah Woe…there is not going to be a union of our bodies. My heart has not accepted you, so I cannot marry you."

Nikpa sighed a deep, prolong sigh.

Aketi turned to Nikpa. "Let my father kill me if he wants to," she said. "I would rather die than follow Tokpah Woe."

Aketi held her hand against her face, expecting Nikpa to hit her again. Nikpa stood staring at her instead, disgustingly. Sianeh pulled her hand from Hawa's grip and covered her open mouth. For a good while, not a single word was spoken. Then, Aketi thought it safe and let down her guard. She was not yet finished.

"As for my mother," Aketi continued, "she has never asked me of my own feelings toward Tokpah Woe. My mother is strongly attached to her customs and happily clings to those old beliefs. I do not understand why she would rather wipe her husband's forehead before her own."

Nikpa furrowed his brow, he had heard enough.

"You are a stupid girl," he shouted furiously. "Where is it wrong for a woman to care for her husband when he is the person taking care of her?"

"With my mother's help, my father has directed my brothers'

26 Liberian slang meaning, consider what you're saying
27 To engage in a sexual relationship

steps to the government school," Aketi said, turning the tables on Nikpa. "Why not my own?" she said to him. "Am I not his child? Why has he not directed my steps to the schoolhouse?"

Nikpa rolled his eyes.

"My mother feels school will lure me away from tradition," Aketi continued. "Isn't it our tradition that measures a woman's worth only by the swelling of her belly? At the same time, having many wives measure her husband's worth. Is it not for the sake of variety a man marries as many women as he wants? Is it not greed? Do you think these women care to share their husbands willingly? The woman is not happy, but our tradition forces her to become a partner to her husband's polygamous ways."

Nikpa stood trembling with anger, staring at Aketi with the utmost disgust.

Aketi broke down crying. "Mama wants to make me like her," she sobbed. "So for my mother's sake, should I leave here and go with Tokpah Woe wearing the face of sadness? Should I walk away from my mother's hut crushing my true feelings beneath my heels? I am not a [28]*kinja*. I am not a basket. I have a heart. I have a mind of my own. Why should my mother pass me from her hand to a man old enough to be my father? Tokpah Woe has chosen me to be his wife, but I have not chosen him to become my husband."

Sianeh raised her hands in protest, but Aketi pressed harder.

"Mama, you must see things as I do," Aketi said. "These men that women obey at the snap of their finger, are they not the ones who work hard so their husbands claim their earnings? The women work hard on the farms while the sun pours heat on their bent backs like fire and at night, their backs ache so dreadfully. Sweat runs down their body for the sake of their husbands...not themselves. His wife gives birth to his children, whose suckling robs her breasts of its round firmness, and then when youth leaves her body and her breasts hang lazy from her chest, this same husband brings in a new wife to take her place. At times, he brings a woman as young as some of his children. Do you think the women love these wives that their husbands marry?"

"I've heard enough!" Nikpa screamed, to the point the veins <u>stood out on the</u> side of his neck. "Who do you think you are? What

28 *A carrying structure or backpack formed by tying palm leaves around a frame of sticks that can be used to transport goods (kola nut, cassava, bananas, palm nuts, charcoal, etc).*

rights have you to disgrace me like this? When did you become my enemy?"

Tokpah Woe shoved both hands into his trousers pockets and tilted his head to the side. He could not believe the girl had shown such disrespect after all he had given her family. Aketi had embarrassed him more than rejected him. All he thought of was, at this point, there was no longer a purpose for any negotiation between him and Nikpa.

"Who are you to give me lectures?" Tokpah Woe said to Aketi, angrily. "Who are you to brush me away like a bothersome fly? You claim not to have a quarrel with me, but you have spoken to me as if I am a dog. I am a man, Aketi! What man would accept such nonsense? You are a foolish woman, trampling on your luck as if it is nothing. My goodness…this woman speaks like one of those liberated women and boasts of reasons to remain one. Even if you beg me like a dog, I will not take you to my home."

"Tokpah Woe, do not say that," Nikpa pleaded.

"You're not going to fool me today, Nikpa," Tokpah Woe said to Nikpa. "The dowry I've paid for your so-called daughter, return every cent to me. Your wife must also give me back the red dress and the money I've given to her. Pack all of my things, everything that I sent by the driver for the celebration…I will leave your village as soon as you give them back to me!"

Tokpah Woe finished and stormed out of the hut.

Nikpa followed him, pleading and begging the marriage take place another day.

"Compromise to a point becomes surrender!" Tokpah Woe shouted at Nikpa's face, pointing his finger.

At any other time, Nikpa would have never allowed it, but his hands were tied. With most of the money spent, and most of the things used, Nikpa stood helpless and could not defend his pride. Tokpah Woe spoke louder and bolder, demanding that his things are returned.

"Nikpa, you should know these things," he challenged. "Has age made you weak? Have you become useless? What man will compromise with that woman? I don't know about you, but I will never heed to a woman!"

"Please, Tokpah Woe, hear what I have to say," Nikpa pleaded.

"No, Nikpa. No! A man's success depends on his wife's backing. How can I take a wife who insists on having her own wishes? Despite what you do, Aketi will not be faithful in her duties. I can do nothing about that. You go and deal with her. I offer Aketi security and a better life, but she has refused them. Go and ask your wife. Sianeh will tell you that many women have wished to be in Aketi's place. The foolish girl wants to go to school as if she is a man. Maybe she wants to be like the women in the pictures. That kind of woman will only bring trouble in my home. I will not take her to my home. Give me back all my money so I can go!"

When Nikpa and Tokpah Woe did not rejoin Oldman Vokai and the others at his nephew's hut, Oldman Vokai left the others to inquire about their long absence. He met Nikpa and Tokpah Woe in the middle of the compound, engaged in their heated disagreement. Oldman Vokai began supervising their argument to bring decorum between the men, switching from side to side in support of each man's viewpoint. Finally, he managed to lessen their argument to a settlement–Tokpah Woe's money would be paid in full at a negotiated time.

After all arrangements were agreed to, Tokpah Woe hired a taxi and left the village. Nikpa left his uncle standing in the middle of the compound and, without thanking him, marched straight to his hut. He pushed the door open and demanded that everyone leaves, also refusing to make clear of his rage. When the last man walked out, Nikpa slammed his door and turned the lock.

No word could have lessened the shame their sister was facing. Hawa and Korto quietly walked out, leaving Sianeh and Aketi in the hut. They went back to the kitchen. Aketi stood staring at her mother; she could not imagine the beating Sianeh was planning to give her.

"Right now, even to speak your name is hard for me," Sianeh said to Aketi. "I will tell you something, Aketi, so listen carefully. The evil you have plotted for me, will not kill me today, it will kill you tomorrow. Are you not one of those children whose sucking robbed my breasts of its firmness? Is this my pay? Aketi, you've paid me with a big shame, to have stood before my family and disgraced me like that. I do not feel as if I am your mother. Had I not given birth to you, I would think otherwise. As sure as the sun comes up in the morning, you will be punished for this. God will make sure of it. One day life will spring a surprise on you, and then you will remember what you've done to me."

Aketi hung her head.

"You cannot even look at me," Sianeh mumbled. "Tell me, who has turned you against me? Leave me alone Aketi…go to the person who has done this ugly thing," Sianeh said and began crying.

Aketi remained standing, feeling sorrow for causing her mother's suffering. Sianeh's words were more hurtful than a few good licks with the new rattan, which Sianeh had retired. It would have been better.

"Did you not hear me?" Sianeh shouted.

Aketi remained standing.

"I say…go!" Sianeh shouted and grabbed Aketi's arm. She shoved Aketi until they were completely out of the hut. "Go! Go!"

Unknown to everyone, Aketi had cleverly repeated what Bendu narrated to her, fueling Aketi's defiance. One day while Aketi sat with Kaela and Teta, Bendu noticed that she had been crying. Bendu sent the girls away to speak to Aketi in private.

"Why have you been crying my daughter?" Bendu asked, but Aketi would not give the reason for her tears, even after a great deal of asking. "I see the source of your distress in your eyes," Bendu said. "A big problem is on your head and it is hard to overcome…it demands a strong will. You'll have to go against the people who have given you life. Am I not correct?"

Aketi made no answer.

"Tell it to me, my daughter, so I can help you," Bendu insisted.

It was then that Aketi confessed she did not want the marriage. The moment seemed perfect for Bendu to share her experience with the girl. She opened her troublesome past to Aketi.

"In my village, when I was young, I was a beautiful girl," Bendu started. "After these years with Nikpa, my beauty has faded from standing over the fire preparing meals that he does not eat because he has already eaten Sianeh's fufu or Dahoe's goat stew. I have made use of my body on his farm while he keeps all the profits. With that money, I cannot buy myself a new lappa without Nikpa's approval. I work hard for the money that he grumbles about spending on me. When I ask him for money for a new one, he gives me lectures on his sons' schooling. He is not happy with the children I've had by him.

All Nikpa does is accuse me of giving him only daughters. Who gives us the children, is it not God? If it were up to me, I would have given him the sons he wants so badly. Enough about me...let's talk about your problem. It seems you do not want the marriage."

"I do not want the marriage," Aketi mumbled.

"Then do not go with it," Bendu suggested. "In the end, you will be left with nothing. You would be like me...a miserable woman all your days, living in despair."

That was the root of Sianeh's so-called plot Aketi did not confess.

Later, Nikpa sent word to the guests the marriage would no longer take place. All preparations had long ended. Mattus, who had witnessed Tokpah Woe leave the village in a rush, assumed there was problem in Nikpa's home. Her proof in the matter was when all the remaining drinks were carried from Nikpa's place. Also, to cover the humiliation Aketi had caused, Sianeh allowed her, and the other women who had come to help with the cooking, take the food home.

When evening came, Nikpa sent for his wives and children. He invited Aketi also, to the surprise of everyone. After the entire family had gathered before Nikpa's front door, he invited everyone to enter his hut except for Aketi, insisting she remain standing in the doorway. Everyone sat down and waited for Nikpa to start the meeting, but Nikpa took his time to present them the situation. The wait was a long and miserable one.

When he was good and ready, Nikpa started with a mind-altering calmness in his voice, "My people, a deep shame is sitting on my heart. It weighs down my entire body...as if a giant rock has been tied around my neck and I've been placed at the deep end of the creek. From today, everyone living in Sass Town will see me as a useless man. What do you think my neighbors will say behind my back? If my own daughter cannot show me respect, who will? Not only has Aketi let loose this pack of scandals after me, she waited until my compound was filled with witnesses to do so. In one day's time, Aketi has thrown away a lifetime's reputation."

Nikpa slowly rose from his seat and walked to where Aketi was standing.

"Your heart is as dark as the moonless night," he said, pointing at Aketi's face. "Regardless of what you have done, I am not the one to appoint your punishment...God will do it for me."

118

Aketi lower her eyes and hung her head.

"You cannot look at me Aketi, because your wickedness is too much," Nikpa scolded. Then he turned to address his wives. "I do not care to know what provoked my daughter to throw away her respect for me. You were all at Sianeh's place and you witnessed how Aketi disinherited me. She chose to disrespect me in front of people because she wants selfhood. Let her have her selfhood. Now it is my term to revolt. I will complete my shame for her."

Nikpa turned to Aketi.

"You are a woman now, so you've shown us," he said. "Go to your mother's place and pack all your belongings...everything. Do not leave out a single item that is yours. At the crack of dawn, take your things and leave my compound...because Aketi, I will no longer accommodate you."

An outburst of weeping came from the family. Teta and Kaela put their arms around each other and howled.

"Why are you crying?" Nikpa screamed at the girls. "Do you want to go with her?"

"No, Paapa...no," the girls mumbled, shaking their heads at the same time. Then their crying quickly changed to sniffles.

Then, Nikpa turned his anger on the rest of the family.

"Anyone who feels sorry for Aketi can follow her," he shouted. "She deserves no pity. Get out, Aketi! Go!"

Nikpa rushed to the door, grabbed Aketi's shoulder, and shoved her until she took a step.

"Get out of my house! When I wake up tomorrow morning, I do not want to see your face around here! Go!"

Aketi marched slowly at first, and then she took off running, appealing to Nikpa in tears, begging that she remain with the family.

"Go! Go!" Nikpa continued shouting.

Dahoe rushed to Nikpa and held his feet. "Find a different punishment for your child, Nikpa. Beat her if you will, but do not throw her away," she begged.

Nikpa glared at her, "I have no listening ears for such compromise," he snarled and pulled his foot away. "In fact, I am finished with you. You all can go now."

In awe of Nikpa's temperament, everyone remained sitting.

"Have you all become deaf? Leave, all of you!" Nikpa shouted.

The women took hold of the younger children's hands and the family leisurely marched out of Nikpa's hut. Yoma and Clay decided to remain behind to give their father support.

"I meant you, too," Nikpa said to his sons with an apologetic tone.

The boys reluctantly walked out. Nikpa slammed his door behind their heels and turned the lock.

Later that evening, all the children joined Aketi in Sianeh's kitchen where she was waiting. This time of the evening is normally spent telling folktales and sharing riddles, but on this night even the warm crackling fire and beautiful moonlight could not create an audience for entertainment. Everyone sat in silence, wondering how Aketi would manage this burden she had brought on herself.

"Kaela…Kaela!"

Kaela heard her mother calling and ran to their hut. She returned to the kitchen after a short while and whispered a message in Aketi's ear. Aketi handed her little bundle to Teta and ran to Bendu's hut.

"Yes, Auntie…you've sent for me?" Aketi greeted Bendu in her doorway, where she was waiting.

"Come inside," Bendu said.

Aketi walked passed Bendu, with downcast eyes, and stopped.

"Dry your eyes my child, this is no time to cry," Bendu said softly. "Worrying is not good…it gives you wrinkles. Follow me."

She led Aketi into her bedroom, put the glowing lantern on the floor beside the bed and sat down. Aketi remained standing.

"Sit by me," Bendu whispered.

Aketi sat down, close to the point of touching. Bendu looked at her and smiled, assuring Aketi her shoulders were there for the girl to lean on.

"I've sent for you so we can talk," Bendu said, still smiling.

"Yes, Aunty," Aketi muttered.

"Aketi, you are a brave little girl. Today you behaved like a [29]*big* woman in our eyes. Who would have dared to go against a man like Nikpa in this town? None of us have that kind of courage. It is as if our tradition has turned women into cowards. Yes, a small girl, not a woman, has shaken this tradition to its core," Bendu said proudly. "Nikpa and Sianeh are vexed with you, but they are not vexed because of the marriage. Do you know why they are vexed?"

---

29 *One worthy of respect*

Aketi shook her head, 'no'.

"They are afraid of the change that is to come. Tradition is like a fabric and we are the common threads that hold it together. When one strand is loose, this fabric can no longer be whole, so everything changes. People do not like change, even when there is much need for it. Our people do not want to accept that whether we like it or not, everything in life must and will change without anyone's approval. It is good to keep your custom, but I believe for a new generation there must be a new method. Some of our customs must change, like marriage. A marriage should be a mutual agreement, but our tradition will not allow it. Is that not wrong?"

"It is wrong, Aunty," Aketi muttered.

"Yes Aketi, it is wrong. You would have never been satisfied living with that man. The marriage was not your choice. Tokpah Woe is too old for you, yet Nikpa and Sianeh wanted the marriage. They wanted the marriage because it is our tradition. Who can blame them? Who in this village have not witnessed a man's greed for power over his wives? The woman cannot turn down her husband when she does not want to make love. He is using her body, should it not be the affairs of the woman to say 'yes' or 'no'? Our tradition forbids the woman to follow her heart, to the point where even our wants are never honored, whether you are wife number one or number twenty-one. Our husband gives each of us our tasks. Can a grown woman not manage well enough on her own without her husband's instructions? Why are we their common property?"

Bendu sucked her teeth.

"Today, your heart is heavy but you will overcome it tomorrow," she continued. "Manage life as you face it Aketi, no matter how difficult it will be."

Then Bendu bend forward, extended her arm as far as she could under her bed, and pulled out a bundle slightly bigger than her fist. She set the little bundle on her lap.

"I am going to help you," she said and pulled loose the knotted tip of the bundle. The bundle opened to a stack of bills, compressed from its longtime togetherness. "Nikpa has warned those who help you, must also follow you. I will help you regardless of his warning. When my husband finds out, he will be vexed with me. Nikpa may never forgive me, but we will find a compromise. Knowing him, it will not be easy, but I will try. I will wait until two days have passed, then I will go and talk to Sianeh. Her heart is hurting now, so she needs some time to heal. Aketi, tell me...what do you want to do now that Nikpa has asked you to leave?"

"I want to go to school with Yoma and Clay," Aketi said, forcing a smile.

"That is not possible," Bendu shook her head. "Nikpa does not want you here and he will not change his mind. Do you want to go to the city?"

"Where, Palm Trees City?"

"Yes...I can send you to my friend, Unady (u-na-day), who lives in Palm Trees City. I have been saving this money to send Kaela, but Kaela has not asked me to send her to school. Nikpa will not allow it and Kaela is not brave. Now that you have stood up to him, I will send you."

Aketi began crying. "Thank you, Aunty," she sobbed.

"Do not cry my daughter," Bendu said. "Go and learn all those things that will enable you to help your sisters. When you have succeeded, remember to help my daughters, okay?"

"Yes, Aunty...I will."

"When you get to the taxi depot in Palm Trees City, ask any of the vendors for Unady. She owes a small [30]cookshop at the taxi depot. Tell Unady that I have sent you to her. You must take her advice and go to school. Learn all those things the boys are learning so they're not better off than you."

"Aunty, one day I will come back for my sisters," Aketi promised.

"God will help you Aketi, you will succeed," Bendu said and rose off her bed.

Aketi stood. "Good-bye, Aunty," she muttered tearfully.

"Good-bye Aketi. Don't forget your sisters," Bendu whispered and pulled Aketi between her shoulders.

Suddenly, the two felt an unexpected kick from Bendu's belly. Aketi stepped back.

"She is saying 'good-bye' to me," Aketi said, smiling.

The two burst out laughing.

Aketi walked out of Bendu's hut, high-spirited once more, and went back to her mother's place.

---

30 A roadside restaurant

It was difficult for everyone starting the day with the usual task as it was no ordinary day. It was foreseeable, considering the unpleasant incident from the day before. Nikpa remained in his hut the entire morning.

Aketi got up before everyone, got dressed, collected her little bundle and was ready to leave. As hard as she tried to get Sianeh's attention, Sianeh did not speak a single word to her daughter.

"Good-bye, Mama," Aketi mumbled to Sianeh and quietly walked out.

With her little bundle tightly secured under her arm, Aketi visited each hut in the compound, except for Nikpa's, to say good-bye. Then she left Nikpa's compound and walked the half-mile distance to the main road to wait for a taxi.

There was no excitement aiming for the world she had wished for and never thought possible. Aketi's heart ached for Nikpa because his ego was not only let down badly, but packed with anger. Also, Sianeh's spirit had been crushed with grief and shame. On top of that, the separation from her sisters put a heavier burden on her. She will not see Kaela and Teta for a longtime to come. Nikpa had accused her of loosening the thread and pulling apart the fabric of their family. Things had fallen apart for good, all because of her selfishness.

However, Aketi managed to find comfort in knowing that because Nikpa and Sianeh's blood ran through her body, regardless of what had happened, she would remain a part of them. Bendu's words were consoling, 'for a new generation, a new method'.

After waiting for an hour or so, Aketi boarded a taxi bounded for Palm Trees City. When the driver took off, she looked back at the road leading back to Nikpa's compound and tears streamed down her cheeks.

"Only the old people belong to their past," Aketi whispered to herself and swapped at her tears.

CRIES OF THE PEPPER BIRDS

The pepper bird, so-called because of its fondness for small scarlet pepper pods, greets the dawn noisily each day. It is their mission in life to wake up the people in the villages, so they believe, and it is at sunrise that these pepper birds are very loud. He claims to be the original alarm clock, not the rooster.

It is told of an old African tale that when the sun drops behind the trees, Father Night gathers all of his tired children in his arms so they can rest from hard work and troubles. They are comforted with many happy dreams during this time. There is also Father Day, who claims these children when the sun rises with each new dawn. This is when the pepper bird perches on Father Night's shoulder and tells him in loud shrieks to release the children to Father Day. So is the mission of the pepper birds throughout the year, during the rainy and dry seasons.

On the west coast of Africa, Liberia is the homeland of the pepper birds. Many of these pepper birds live in [1]*Bong County* where the [2]*Kpelle* people live. Not so far in Bong County sits the beautiful village of Sinta, where the life of the village and activities of the tropical forest go on peacefully. High in trees sit chattering monkeys, shyly peeping from behind giant banana tree leaves. Early in the evening during the dry season, big-eye bummy fish crawl out of shallow waters onto the mud. And, the giant mango tree near the village is for sure the gathering place of every pepper bird. Most folks in Sinta are up at the crack of dawn, but the pepper birds get up before all.

On the last night of the dry season, the silver moon had a soft gleam.

---

1 *One of 15 counties in Liberia, where the Kpelle tribe lives; Gbanga is the capital city.*
2 *A tribe in Liberia, West Africa*

It hung full and beautiful as morning came gradually. Garpue, a prominent member of this bird society, woke up first. She stretched her wings as far out as she could stretch them and shook off the nightlong rest.

"Korlu-oooooh, are you awake?" Garpue called her little bird while she slept warm and comfortably in the nest.

"Not yet Mother," Korlu chirped drowsily. "It's too early to get up. It is not yet dawn."

"But we, pepper birds, get up before all," Garpue cried. "Get up, Korlu, get up now! We must be ready to join the others in our cries."

The little pepper bird opened her eyes halfway, peeped at her mother, and shut them again.

Not again, Garpue thought and prepared her speech. For the umpteenth time she was going to remind Korlu of an important responsibility Korlu had purposely ignored learning.

"Have you thought about learning to fly?" Garpue asked. "Do you not know it is important that you learn to fly?"

"Mother, I'm afraid of heights," Korlu repeated her same excuse.

"Today, it is 'heights'. What will it be tomorrow? What new excuse will you use? Birds are not afraid of heights...we live in trees. We fly to places most animals wish they could visit and we watch people work and go about their business. Need I go on? Besides, how would you survive if you cannot fly?"

Korlu thought it over for a moment and then she tweeted, "I'll live here with you, Mother! I can take care of the nest while you are away."

Garpue chuckled, but it was not a pleasing chuckle.

"Why do you keep making these excuses?" She quarreled. "How would you survive? How would you feed your little babies?"

"I have no babies," Korlu said, giggling.

"You will, someday. How will you feed them then?"

"I won't have any babies, Mother, I promised."

"What about food? How would you eat?"

"You always share your food with me, Mother."

"What about a home of your own? How would you build a nest if you cannot fly?"

"I won't need a nest, Mother…I'll live here with you. See, Mother, I will be just fine. Oh Mother," Korlu tweeted cheerfully, "I will stay right here with you…you will never be lonely."

"Korlu, I can no longer accept your excuses," Garpue shrieked. "You must learn to fly…a bird's survival depends on it."

Except for Korlu, all of Garpue's other baby pepper birds had learned to fly and had, in fact, built nests of their own; either on the giant mango tree branch or on another branch somewhere. The only thing Korlu cared about was joining the pepper bird community at dawn. She wanted to chirp the loudest when they united in their cries to wake the villagers.

"Okay, Mother…I will learn to fly," Korlu promised, halfheartedly.

When it was dawn, Korlu pointed her beak toward the sky and chirped to her heart's content. As soon as the pepper birds were done, Garpue took to the air; just Korlu was left alone in the nest.

How hard can flying lessons be? Korlu thought. *I will take a nap while Mother is gone. When she gets back, I'll be well rested.*

Korlu dozed off in a short time. All morning long she went through a spell of short naps. Now and then, Korlu would open her teeny-weeny eyes to peep at the sun, but the sun was late in rising. In fact, the bright sun never came up.

Suddenly, a teasing yank on the tree branch shifted Garpue's nest and rocked it slightly to one side. The nest had not moved much to build a concern, until a cold droplet tapped Korlu's beak. She opened her eyes and looked up. The sky was dark. It seemed as though it was nighttime again although there was not a twinkling star in sight. Even the beautiful pearl blue moon was missing.

Korlu decided to sleep a little longer when a sudden clap of thunder exploded! Her eyes flashed wide open. Then a gusty wind came whirling across the forest, wrecking every tree in its path. Heavy rain started and mixed with it was thundering. At the end of each clap of thunder, long lines of lightning flashed across the sky. Every time the thunder sounded, Korlu would shove her toes deeper into the floor of their nest. Soon she began shivering from the pouring rain that had soaked her body.

Then, a boom-splintering blast sounded!

The mango tree shook, crackled, and then tilted. Garpue's nest airborne in a flash, and was whisked off the branch. It traveled a short distance before landing near the edge of Kandea Creek and Korlu landed hard alongside it. Frighten out of her wits, she hopped underneath the lop-sided nest and in a little while, Korlu fell fast to sleep while waiting for the rain to stop.

"Hello little one," a friendly voice chatted.

Korlu opened her eyes and there he was, an odd-looking creature sitting on the water, starring at her with the most beautiful set of sparkling eyes she had ever seen.

"My name is Old Dwe," the duck shouted from the creek. "What's yours?"

Korlu came out from underneath the lop-sided nest, eager to meet him, and then hopped toward the creek. She reached a safe enough distance from the edge of the water and stopped. Old Dwe's mirrored image in the water seemed puzzling.

"What is your name?" Old Dwe asked again.

"Korlu," the little pepper bird replied and asked, "Have you seen my mother?"

Poor eyesight prevented Old Dwe from seeing the bird, so he swam closer to the water edge. "Ah...a pepper bird...what did you say your name was?"

"Korlu," she repeated. "Have you seen my mother?"

"I have not seen your mother. In fact, I haven't seen much of anything lately. Why would your mother come near the creek on such a beautiful day? She must be enjoying the view somewhere. Why aren't you flying with her?"

"I don't know how to fly."

"You don't know how to fly?" Old Dwe asked, surprised. Then he turned to a few ducks that had, in a short time, joined him. "Hey friends, listen up! This little bird tells me she does not know how to fly. Have any of you ever met a bird that does not know how to fly? I've never seen such oddness in my days."

All the ducks exploded in delirious laughter. Old Dwe laughed so hard he nearly fell over.

"Why didn't her mother teach her to fly?" asked one of the ducks.

"Surely her mother must have taught her. How did she get here?" Old Dwe said to the duck.

"The wind blew down our nest," Korlu explained. "I was left at home to care for the nest when a giant wind came and blew it down. I came right with it."

"It must have been the storm that passed through the area this morning, remember? That was the reason we flew to the next town," Old Dwe reminded the other ducks.

"That storm blew our nest off the tree branch and I landed here," Korlu said. "See the nest?" She pointed at the lop-sided nest.

"Where will you live?" Old Dwe asked. "You will have to build another nest, but how could you? You do not know how to fly."

"I can live here with you and be a duck," Korlu suggested. "Can I?"

Old Dwe chuckled.

"That cannot be, Korlu, you cannot be a duck," he said. "Shouldn't you be with the other pepper birds when they wake the villagers?"

"I should be, shouldn't I? But, Old Dwe, I can no longer be a pepper bird...I don't know how to fly. I *have* to be a duck."

"A pepper bird can never be a duck," Old Dwe shook his head. Then he quickly swam to the edge of the creek, climbed up to the shore, wobbled to where Korlu was standing and stopped. "Look at your feet," he pointed.

Korlu looked at her feet.

"See what I mean?" Old Dwe said.

"No…what's wrong with my feet?"

"Nothing is wrong with your feet…if you are a bird. If you want to be a duck, those feet are wrong for you."

"Why are they wrong?"

"Your toes are not webbed. How would you swim? Pepper birds are not swimmers. I could carry you around on my back, but I couldn't do that all day. Besides, if you fall into the water, you'd drown."

"Drown? I…I don't want to drown," Korlu cried.

"Don't worry my little friend, I wouldn't let you. In fact, I have an idea!"

Being the oldest duck in the waterfowl community, Old Dwe was wiser than most. Throughout three generations of ducks, he had the proper understanding of everything. The ducks trusted his judgments in all matters.

"Every one of us listen to Old Dwe...he's wise and he knows everything," the group of ducks quacked.

"Well then, Korlu, you *could* live with the chickens!" Old Dwe announced proudly.

Korlu's face lit up. "My mother told me stories about the chickens! Where do they live? I want to live with them!"

"Follow that road!" Old Dwe pointed at the narrow road, wide enough only for foot traffic. The dirt path led direct towards a giant *bug-a-bug* mount.

"Great! That's not so far from the creek. I can visit you as often as I like."

"The chickens do not live there," Old Dwe corrected quickly. "They live in Sinta, a little village pass the mount."

"Well, just how far is Sinta?" Korlu asked.

"Sinta is not that far away, if you can fly," Old Dwe said, and then he told his brilliant facts. "The village is a small one; it is made up of six huts closely packed together in no plain order. There is a small shed near the hut, which the people use for their *kitchen*. This shed has no walls. You can always find something to eat while the women are cooking. Then, there is a big square hut where rice is stored. When the rice has ripened, the people cut it and carry it in large bundles on their heads. They tote the rice bundles from the farm straight to the village and store them in this square hut."

"Wow," Korlu tweeted happily. She could hardly wait to meet with the chickens.

"There is also a long hut built with barbwires," Old Dwe continued. "This is where the chickens live. They are a friendly brood so they will be glad to have you live with them. Who knows, they may even teach you to be a chicken. You do look like them, only a bit smaller. Be sure to tell them Old Dwe send you."

"I sure will," Korlu tweeted and did a frisky hop. "I'm ready to meet the chickens."

"You're excited about meeting the chickens and all, but don't go near the big square hut," Old Dwe warned. "If you do, the village people will run you off. Some may even throw stones at you."

"Why? Is it because those people are selfish?"

"Selfish? No, they are not selfish. They drive the fowls away because fowls are notorious for pecking grains."

"Shouldn't they share their rice?"

"Share their rice with the chickens! No, no, no," Old Dwe cried. Then he whispered, "The rice is only shared among the people. Part of it is eaten and part of it is sold at the market. Harvesting rice is hard work. First, the people clear the land by cutting away the bushes before planting. When the brush is dried, they burned it. Those people spend long hours stooping over muddy paddies to plant one seedling at a time. While the rice is growing, they have to weed the entire farm by getting rid of unwanted plants. Besides working so hard, they have to drive away your rice-eating cousins to protect their harvest.

"Planting is just part of it," Old Dwe continued. "When it is time to reap their crop, the entire village goes to the rice farm early in the morning. All the adults get in the rice field while the drummers remain sitting at the edge of the farm. People in all ages and sizes form a line, standing shoulder-to-shoulder, across the rice field. Their leader would order a command in a loud voice, and gathered from his wave, the people move together to the rhythm of the drums. Mind you, a speedy reaper is as much a bother as a slow reaper. Either one spoils the rhythm. They move as one in a spectacular order. Some of the people follow the cutters to collect the rice bunch, take them to the edge of the farm, and tie them together. Later, these big bunches of rice are carried to the village and stored in the square hut."

"That is hard work," Korlu agreed. "I'm tired just hearing about it."

"Hard work indeed…Kpelle people are hard workers. They seem happy while they're working. There is always laughter and singing while they are in the rice field. Do you know why?"

"No," Korlu replied.

"The people built their strength in uniting," Old Dwe explained. "Their work becomes manageable with the vibrations of the drum-beats when they come together."

"Old Dwe, you are a clever duck," Korlu said. "It would have been better for me to stay here with you, don't you think?"

"I would love to have you stay with us, Korlu, but go on to the village. The creek is no place for a pepper bird. Leave now so you can reach Sinta before dark. Remember [3]Good-friend, you must not go near the storage hut."

"I won't go near it. Good-bye, Old Dwe," Korlu twittered and started towards the termite mount.

Korlu did not think about stopping to rest, being eager to meet the chickens. Her quick springy hops carried her farther away from the creek. Soon, she could no longer see Old Dwe and the other ducks.

"Hello, there!" a rasping voice chatted.

Korlu stopped. She looked to her left and then to her right. She looked behind, but saw only the green bushes that were railing both sides of the road. "I cannot see you. Where are you?" she asked.

"Here," the voice chatted from behind the bushes. He poked out his head at first, and then came his long artistic-designed body.

Blown away by the serpent's odd brownish markings, Korlu stood staring at his beautiful pattern.

"Where are you going?" the serpent asked.

But before Korlu could make an answer, a gusty wind swooped over her and the boa, nearly knocking her over. She managed to look up and there he was, Toimu, the famous hawk Garpue had bragged knowing. Toimu dashed toward the ground so fast that Korlu had no time to say hello or ask whether he had seen Garpue. In a spell of a moment, the giant hawk was flying through the sky carrying the long wiggling boa between his claws. Korlu wondered why Toimu was in such hurry. She waited until he had flown out of sight and

---

3 *To address a stranger in a friendly manner*

then started back on her journey.

Korlu reached the six-foot bug-a-bug mount and close to the mount was a caravan of worker ants marching in a near perfect procession, drilling energetically with the last bits of food that had been gathered after the thunderstorm.

"Have you seen my mother?" Korlu shouted at the ants.

Not a single ant answered. The ants kept marching. She thought of asking them for some food; seemingly, not an ant was willing to break his strides. She left them alone and hopped by.

Korlu passed a few nervous earthworms, three float-away butter-flies, and a couple of jumping crickets. Except for the ducks and boa, everyone seemed too busy to chitchat.

Finally, Korlu reached Sinta!

From the outskirt of the neatly kept village, she waited between the tall green grasses as their friendly slender leaves bent back and forth in the cool late afternoon breeze. The first hut she intended finding was the kitchen. If the people were cooking, as wise Old Dwe had said, she would find something to eat. Korlu spotted the kitchen across the yard.

She hurried her hops over perfectly placed broom tracks until she reached the kitchen. It was bare and deserted. In fact, the whole village seemed quiet except for the squabbling noise at the other side, where the chicken coop was. She rushed over to see what was happening. Next to the coop, a little village boy, about twelve years old, was throwing seeds at the ground while the chickens pecked at them. After the boy emptied his bucket and walked away, Korlu hopped closer to the chickens and stopped.

"Hello everyone, my name is Korlu," she greeted the chickens. "Can I be a chicken and live here with you?"

The chickens stopped and every fowl exploded into hilarious laughter–belly shaking laughs.

"Oh dear me," laughed Lurpu, a beautiful red hen. "This little pepper bird is amusing. Tell me, little one, why would a pepper bird want to be a chicken?"

"Old Dwe said that I could live as a chicken," Korlu said. "Do you know Old Dwe?"

"Yes, the old duck at Kandea Creek," Lurpu replied. "Why would he suggest such a thing? You are not a chicken."

"I want to be a chicken...only until I find my mother."

"Find your mother? Why would your mother leave you?" Lurpu asked.

"She did not leave me. Early this morning while she was out finding food for us, the wind blew down our nest. I have not seen her since," Korlu explained. "I don't know where she is or where to look. Our nest was blown to shreds, now I don't have a place to live. Can I live here with you?"

"That Old Dwe is a clever one...sending a pepper bird to the chickens," Lurpu chuckled. "I am sorry little one, but you cannot be a chicken. You are a pepper bird."

"But I have to be a chicken...I have nowhere to live," Korlu said.

She hopped to the hen, close to touching, and looked at Lurpu from head to toe.

"What are you doing?" Lurpu asked.

"I'm looking at you," Korlu replied.

"Why are you looking at me?"

"I am looking at your feathers. I see that you have wings. You also have a bill, don't you?"

"Well, I do have a beak...and I have beautiful red feathers," Lurpu bragged.

"May I ask one more question?" Korlu said.

"Go ahead."

"Are you a chicken or are you a bird?"

Lurpu thought things over for a moment. "It seemed like a trick question," she said. "However, I will answer you...I am a chicken."

"You are a bird as well," Korlu said.

Lurpu laughed. "I knew it was a trick question," she giggled. "Well...I guess I am a bird also."

"Can't I be a bird and a chicken?"

"Korlu, you are not a fowl," Lurpu insisted. "You are a pepper bird."

"I cannot be a duck because I cannot swim. I cannot be a hawk because I cannot fly. Why can't I be a chicken until I find my mother?" Korlu whined. "I'd like to live here with you on the farm, can I?"

"Did you just say, 'You cannot fly'?" Lurpu cried, surprised. "You are a bird...all birds know how to fly!" Then she turned to the arrogant rooster that was feeding nearby. "Hey Yarkpawolo, don't all birds know how to fly?"

Yarkpawolo laughed rather than answer. He looked at the little pepper bird, shook his head, and went back to eating.

Lurpu wanted his attention anyway. "It is like saying Yarkpawolo does not know how to crow," she announced. "We know how he brags about being a rooster. He even sings his name when he is crowing, *Yar-kpa-wolo, Yar-kpa-wolo*," she sang.

All the chickens giggled to Lurpu's playful ridicule.

Then one of the chickens teased further, "Yarkpawolo, this little pepper bird wants to be a chicken."

Yarkpawolo looked at Korlu. "But you're a pepper birrrrrd," he mocked.

All the chickens laughed, they knew about the rooster's strong dislike for pepper birds. For a longtime Yarkpawolo felt cheated the pepper birds had stolen his title, the village timepiece. Now with an opportunity at hand, it would be a perfect revenge to show off in front of his rival. Yarkpawolo playfully ruffled his feathers around his neck, to amuse the chickens, and strutted like a peacock. The chickens laughed harder, some nearly choke on the seeds they were eating. Only Lurpu did not like the treatment of their guest.

"She is our guest, so we must *all* be nice to her," Lurpu advised. Then she scolded Yarkpawolo with a stern, but friendly, stare.

"I didn't invite her here," Yarkpawolo taunted.

"None of us did," Lurpu replied. Then she turned to the rest of the chickens. "Can Korlu stay with us until her mother comes to find her?" she asked. "I think she should stay...what do you think?"

"Well, sure she can stay," replied one chicken.

"Yes," said another.

Soon, every fowl agreed for Korlu to stay with them.

"But you must warn her," suggested the first chicken.

Lurpu was not sure of what she was to warn Korlu.

"You better warn her about you-know-who," Yarkpawolo advised, he had suddenly rejoined the brood.

Without thinking, Lurpu said to Korlu, "Do not go near the big square hut."

"Not that," Yarkpawolo quickly corrected.

Lurpu could not think of anything else.

The rest of the chickens shouted in harmony, "Garmenh!"

"I forgot all about him," Lurpu chuckled. "Yes, Korlu, I must warn you."

"Who is Garmenh?" Korlu asked.

"Yeekie's stupid cat," Yarkpawolo said. Just then, he saw the white tomcat trailing after the boy. "He follows Yeekie everywhere," he added, with envy.

"Garmenh gives us a good chase every time," Lurpu advised, still giggling. "He chases us as often as four or five times a day. I've never seen him catch a chicken yet. We fly to places where he cannot reach us. Some of us fly to the roof of the huts. Some fly up the pawpaw trees. We fly away as far as we can."

"That's right, Korlu. Go ahead and form a group with the hens," Yarkpawolo teased. "Birds of the same feathers do flock together. Personally, I do not want a pepper bird hanging around me. I have an image to keep. Besides, Garmenh knows better than to give me a chase."

"Never mind that rooster," Lurpu interrupted Yarkpawolo. "Korlu, you can stay with us. Now, get some seeds before they are all gone. Yarkpawolo pecks faster than any fowl I know."

"I sure do," Yarkpawolo bragged. "And, I am not about to stop."

Korlu was happy to join the chickens. She tried copying their method of eating, but could not find a single grain. In fact, she was not able to eat at all. Korlu gave up trying and stood watching the chickens.

"Just don't stand there," Lurpu warned her. "All these seeds would be gone before you know it. Don't you want any?"

"I do, but I can't find any of the seeds. Where are they?"

"Right in front of you...the seeds are everywhere. You'll have to scratch before you peck," Lurpu said.

"How do I do that? I've tried, but I'm not able to scratch."

"Run your toes through the dirt so you can uncover the seeds. Much of the seeds are buried in the sand. You have to uncover them," Lurpu explained.

Korlu moved one foot forward and tried to copy Lurpu's example, but she did not know how to drag her foot back. It seemed stuck forward. "I don't know how to scratch," she complained.

"Watch me," Lurpu suggested and toed the spot in front of her. Then she scraped the ground with her nails, digging one foot, and then the other. There were bits of grains everywhere. "There they are, see them?" she said. "You have to scratch so you can find the seeds. After that, you have to peck at them with your beak."

"Let me try," Korlu said, after watching keenly.

Korlu moved her foot forward, but had a hard time pulling it back.

Watching the little pepper bird struggle with the task, Yarkpawolo laughed. "Korlu is not a chicken," he teased.

It seemed best to separate Yarkpawolo from the rest of the chickens, Lurpu playfully chased him away.

"Lurpu has become a mother hen to a pepper bird," Yarkpawolo went on teasing. "Don't call me when Garmenh comes chasing you around!"

"I am a bird, Yarkpawolo...and so are you," Lurpu yelled back.

"I am a rooster...I am a rooster," Yarkpawolo bragged as he strutted away.

The chickens were so busy pecking at the seeds that not one chicken notice Garmenh as he crept toward them. Garmenh calculated his steps, between him and the closest chicken, mapping and planning his attack. All that time, not one chicken noticed him. He reached within a good striking distance and stopped. Garmenh stretched his hind legs as far back as they could go, to put his plan into motion, and then lowered his front legs as close to the ground as possible. It was Lurpu that spotted him as soon as he was ready to make his move.

"Here comes Garmenh!" Lurpu alerted the chickens.

Garmenh leaped toward the chickens and they all scattered and flew in different directions. Normally, Garmenh does not commit to one chase. While he chases a fowl, another seemed closer. He constantly abandons one chase for another.

Some chickens flew up to the branches of a tall tree nearby, to hide among the thick foliage. Some went flying to the roof of the hut. Only Korlu remained standing.

"Fly away, Korlu, he won't catch you," Lurpu warned.

Just then, Garmenh noticed the bird and deserted all other chase. He slid toward Korlu, hung his giant paw over her, and in a split second, pushed her down until her belly was almost touching the ground.

"Yarkpawolo, come quickly!" Lurpu yelled. "Garmenh has caught Korlu! Do something, Yarkpawolo, do something!"

Yarkpawolo stopped in his tracks when he heard Lurpu's pleading. He turned around, although he had promised not to, and dashed toward Garmenh. Yarkpawolo reached near Garmenh and halted, leaving long footprints in the dirt. "Let her go!" he demanded.

Garmenh took hold of Korlu with his mouth and waited, tempting the rooster to a dare.

"Put the bird down!" Yarkpawolo demanded again.

Garmenh crept back. He had not done so out of fear, it was to provoke a fight, as all their previous fights started in this manner. Yarkpawolo waited. Garmenh took another step back, wanting to fight.

While tension mounted between the rooster and the cat, the rest of the chickens sat watching from their individual hiding places. Yarkpawolo would have waited for Garmenh to make his move, but Korlu's loud twittering pushed him into starting the fight. He leaped toward Garmenh with perfect timing and started the fight.

This caused an outburst of squawking from the chickens. There were scattered clouds of red dust swirling everywhere as the chickens flew down from their different towering places. Yeekie noticed the dust and sprinted to the scene. When he got there, Garmenh saw him and immediately released his jaws. Korlu fell fast to the ground.

"Korlu does not know how to fly," Lurpu said to the other chickens, after they had settled down. "See...she didn't fly away with us."

"But, she's a bird," replied one of the chickens.

"All birds should be able to fly," said another.

Yeekie picked up the bird and began stroking her head to calm her, but Korlu continued to shake even after many gentle strokes. Then he thought of another idea and took off running. Garmenh chased his heels, stride for stride, all the way to the family hut.

Yeekie reached the hut, found the new bamboo basket his mother had just finished and placed Korlu in it. He ran to the storage hut, with the basket secured in his hand, and went in. Yeekie found a suitable place on the shelf beneath the ceiling and set the basket down. When Korlu noticed the strings of fresh-cut rice heads sticking out the palm thatch ceiling, she knew she had broken her promise–she had entered the forbidden hut!

"I promised Old Dwe I will not go to the storage hut," Korlu shrieked. "Please, don't leave me in here! Take me out! Take me out!"

Korlu's loud twittering from the storage hut alerted the chickens. Lurpu looked at Yarkpawolo, as if it seemed right to break the rule.

"Don't you dare go into that hut," Yarkpawolo warned her.

To Lurpu, it was no time to obey the rules. She left Yarkpawolo standing and went marching toward the forbidden hut. Yarkpawolo, reluctantly, followed.

Yeekie spotted the chickens as they crept by the door, but chose to ignore them. His involvement with the bird was more important than driving away two hardheaded chickens. As long as they remained outdoors, he would not bother them.

Yeekie inspected Korlu's wings, carefully looking for cuts or bruises. There were neither cuts nor bruises. In fact, there were no injuries as far as he could tell. Then to find out whether the bird could fly, he threw her high above his head.

"Fly away little one," Yeekie shouted.

Korlu tugged her wings and shut her eyes as her little body zoomed toward the ceiling. She stayed in the air only for a little while, and then came falling towards the ground, landing hard on the stack of rice bundles that had been left from the day before. Yeekie hurriedly picked her up. He started to throw Korlu in the air a second time, but stopped at his mother's calling. He put Korlu back in the basket, checked the door latch to make sure it was lock, and ran back to the family hut. Garmenh followed.

Lurpu strode near the doorway when she thought it was safe. "Korlu, are you all right," she called.

"Up here, Lurpu, up here," Korlu tweeted.

Lurpu looked up and saw the basket on the shelf. Korlu was in big trouble, she thought. Many chickens in Sinta had disappeared and all the chickens were aware of it. Every time a fowl or some other small farm animal was placed in one of those baskets, they were never seen again. For a longtime, a tale had hung around their coop the village people took the animals to the market, in those baskets, and exchanged them for money.

Lurpu did not have much time to think things over. She looked to her left and then to her right, not a single village person was in sight. Against Yarkpawolo's stern warning, she sly stepped into the forbidden hut, flew to the edge of the ceiling, and easily landed next to the basket. Yarkpawolo left the forbidden hut and sprinted back to the chicken coop.

"How did you do it?" Korlu asked Lurpu as soon as she landed.

"I flew up," Lurpu said. "Now, listen to me Korlu, listen keenly… this is important. If you decide to be a chicken, you must learn to fly. Every time Garmenh chases us around, she will catch you. You might not be so lucky next time."

"This is no luck," Korlu said. "It is no fun being locked up in a cage. I'll never be able to fly."

"You must learn to fly," Lurpu insisted, "you must. You have not even tried. Never give up without first trying."

"There's no room in the basket," Korlu said, looking around. "The ceiling is low...the basket is small…."

"Stop making excuses," Lurpu cried. "No matter how hard it seem, you must learn to fly."

"How can I learn to fly while I'm locked up?"

"You can learn," Lurpu said.

"But, how?"

"I am going to teach you," Lurpu said, firmly.

"Teach me to fly? I'd like to see that."

"Yes, Korlu, you can learn to fly while you are in the basket. When Yeekie comes back and take you out of the basket, you'll be able to fly away. All you have to do is watch me. Do what I do, okay?"

"Okay," Korlu mumbled.

Lurpu spread her wings and quickly took to the air. In a short time, she was landing next to the bundle of rice. "Did you see that?" she shouted.

"No, I didn't," Korlu said. "You were too fast...I didn't see a thing."

Lurpu flew back to the shelf and landed next to the basket. "You must watch me closely," she warned.

Lurpu took to the air and like before, she landed next to the bundle of rice.

"I did not see a thing," Korlu grumbled, as soon as Lurpu landed.

Lurpu flew back to the basket, landed close by it and poked her beak at the small opening near the basket door. "I will show you what I did, Korlu," she said. "I spread my wings and flapped them...as I was flapping them, I leaped into the air. Go ahead and try it. Flap your wings like I did mine."

"How do I flap my wings?"

"Like this," Lurpu said, waving her wings up and down. She did it over and over, at a speed Korlu could easily follow.

"Like this?" Korlu asked, copying closely.

"That's it! Go faster! Faster! Now, jump into the air. Jump up while you flap. Do it faster!" Lurpu shouted.

Korlu moved her wings up and down, as fast as she was able to.

"Push your body up...off the basket floor. Do it now, Korlu! Do it!" Lurpu cheered.

Korlu moved her wings faster. Then, suddenly, she felt her tiny body lift off the basket floor. Soon Korlu was near the top.

"Lurpu, I am flying," Korlu cried.

Unaware, Korlu had pushed herself a little higher than expected. Her head slammed against the basket ceiling, but it was not a hurtful hit.

"Korlu, you were flying," Lurpu said and burst out laughing. "Keep flying until you are able to control your body. Soon you will be able to fly away from Garmenh...even further!"

Then, Lurpu coached Korlu in every method of flying. Soon Korlu was flying, easily managing the small space inside the bamboo basket.

"I'll go and tell the others," Lurpu said and flew down to the floor. She dashed out the door, as fast as her feet carried her, and sprinted to the coop. "Korlu is flying! Korlu is flying!" Lurpu announced the news.

"I can't believe it," Yarkpawolo crowed. "That little pepper bird does not know how to fly."

"I taught her how to fly," Lurpu said, "I did."

"I do not believe it," Yarkpawolo argued.

"I watched her fly around the basket," Lurpu insisted.

"Well, we'll just have to find out next time Garmenh chase you around," Yarkpawolo crowed and went back into the coop.

Back at the storage hut, Korlu flew around and around in the basket until she got tired. She could not wait to find her mother and showoff her new skills. Best of all, she planned on flying into the world like the other pepper birds. After the early morning shrieks, Korlu planned to explore the scenery she had only heard about. She wanted to see the high hills that were dressed with goats and sheep, the natural stream of water much larger than Kandea Creek, and especially the colorful croplands; the orange groves, the cabbage patch and cornfields.

All the villagers had returned from their farms by sundown, but Yeekie had not come back to the hut. Mixed with the people chattering were pounding noises the women made while maneuvering the pestle in the mortar as they prepared food for cooking. The scent from the boiling pots was for sure the proof of dinnertime. Korlu would have easily found something to eat, but she was sitting in a locked bamboo basket tired and hungry.

The village gradually got quiet as time went on.

Suddenly, Korlu heard Garmenh meow. His meowing got clearer and closer and then, from nowhere, he crept in the doorway and looked up. At the same time, the thumping noise of running feet followed; Yeekie bust through the door with a group of small boys. He led them to the basket, chattering his promised surprise for the boys. Korlu watched Yeekie's hands as he went to unlatch the door, calculating a perfect timing for her flight. As soon as he unlatched the door and open it, Korlu jetted out.

"I've taught the bird to fly," Yeekie bragged to his friends. "See...I told you I found a bird...I taught her how to fly!"

Korlu flew from the basket, aimed for the doorway and flew straight through it. The boys ran out to see where she was heading to. Korlu flew toward the chicken coop.

"Lurpu...Yarkpawolo...I'm going to find my mother," Korlu chirped as she reached the chicken coop.

Lurpu, Yarkpawolo and many of the chickens rushed out of the coop, just in time to see Korlu fly over.

"Good-bye, Korlu," Lurpu waved.

"Good-bye, everybody," Korlu tweeted and soared over the coop.

Korlu flew over Sinta, passed the bug-a-bug mount, and in a short time, reached Kandea Creek. She spotted Old Dwe sitting on the water with a few ducks.

"Good-bye Old Dwe," she tweeted from the sky.

Old Dwe looked up and saw Korlu soaring over his head like a pro.

"Korlu, is that you?" he asked.

"Yes, Old Dwe, it's me. I can fly! I can fly!"

"I thought you wanted to be a chicken?"

"Oh no, Old Dwe, I do not want to be a chicken. I am a pepper bird."

"You are a pepper bird," Old Dwe said.

"Yes, I am...I must join the others before daybreak...I want to chirp the loudest when we sound the alarm for the villagers. So long

Old Dwe!"

"Good-bye Korlu," Old Dwe waved.

Korlu glided over Kandea Creek, and then into the golden sunset in search of her family.

LOOKING FOR A GOOD READ?
Heart Men by Ophelia S. Lewis

RJ's fight against injustice for victims, especially women, made him one of the best lawyers in Atlanta. He had everything an ambitious young lawyer could want; a promising career and a beautiful fiancée he'd promise to love forever, Dr. Gia Ricciola. Trouble comes when his father, Senator Robert J. Douglas II, is arrested for ritualistic murder in Liberia. RJ is wide-eyed to the struggle of life in terms of change in post civil war Liberia—justice for all and the nation's biggest problem, the sexual exploitation of women. But in the process of helping with his father's defense, his eyes are opened to the rituals of the heart man who kills for human parts. Even as RJ sought to condemn the depravity of the society's social sins, in the darkest hour of the trial, he is tempted into an affair with the legal assistant and is forced to judge his own conscience.

Publisher: Village Tales Publishing
Format: Paperback and eBook
ISBN: 978-0-9753609-6-5
eISBN: 978-0-9753609-9-6

Print and eBook
Available from Amazon.com
and other retail outlets
Available on Kindle & other devices

More titles at
www.villagetalespublishing.com

READ ALL THE HEART MEN BOOKS

HEART MEN (a novel)
Paperback / 244 Pages / 2011
ISBN 13: 9780975360965
eBook ISBN: 9780975360996

DEAD GODS (HM2)
Paperback / 396 Pages / 2014
ISBN 13: 9780978362522
eBook ISBN: 9780978362539

READERS REVIEWS

"I am REALLY ENJOYING Heart Men..."—*Richelle Howell*

"Overall, HEART MEN is an INTERESTING read...I ENJOYED RJ's PASSION for life, his LOVE for his family, and his tenacious search for the TRUTH...I certainly enjoyed his story. It held my interest from beginning to end."—Damali Griffin (Imani Literary Group Book Club Member)

"This is a story that has NEVER BEEN TOLD...I was pleasantly surprised to find out it is a LOVE STORY more than anything..."—Manseen Logan (Bella Beau Marketing & Publicity)

"I just finished reading HEART MEN here in Ghana on my Kindle...I LIKED IT A LOT...It seems that there are so many TABOO SUBJECTS in a society, and this is one not just in Liberia but everywhere...—Tim Nevin

A picture book that offers a unique way to teach young children good manners using the 26 letters of the alphabets we all know. Each letter of the alphabet is represented, relating to teaching social standards with the principles of right conduct and good manner. Recommended for children ages 3 and up. Every parent should use this book, and every teacher too.

ISBN: 9780985362515
eISBN: 9780985362553
Print and eBook
Available from Amazon.com and
other retail outlets
Available on Kindle and other devices

Also available in 24 x 36
Jumbo Poster
www.villagetalespublishing.com

Read on for an excerpt from DEAD GODS (HM2)
By Ophelia S. Lewis

1
꙳ᢀᢀ꙳

The world connects at lightning speed, but things were still as if it was 1986 in Liberia. After 15 years of civil war and six years of an elected presidency, progress was painfully slow. Although the cellular phone was booming and substantially more widespread than fixed line telephonic transmission, technology was otherwise, creeping out of the Stone Age in Monrovia—a city police department without computers on every detective's desk, and a wish list of working fax machines and photocopiers needed for critical documents. Forget quick access to DNA technology. Some would admit fingerprint was still being matched by human eye. All this is hard to gasp in today's CSI effect, but it is what it is.

His pay is not the biggest pay, his job is not the easiest, but Officer Lonos is a man who would rather die for his principals than live without one. He accepted the occupation as an officer knowing the responsibilities and hazards involved. As far as he was concerned, hell was not large enough for heart-men. Based on the most recent crime scene, it was evident the heart-men had struck again.

Behavior science never changes, so criminal profiling is still a quick thinker's investigative tool. For the detective in such environment, criminal profiling is always brought to the forefront of law enforcement. For one thing, such crime involves co-conspirators who could keep secrets. Secondly, logistics, the means of transportation. Getting from point A to point B increases having to be neat and discreet. Then, lodging the victim. They had to put their victim where extraction is done without drawing attention. Disposal was the final and easier step, Liberia's shorelines, the beaches.

As far as Lonos was concerned, Aaron Dolo had only done

enough for his conscience to feel as if he had done something. The police chief had not done nearly enough because CeRue Manor, the mastermind behind most of the mishap in Monrovia, was still a loose thread.

It was no wonder that some consider victims of the heart-man unlucky. Murdering for human parts is a peculiar wicked deed, but a heart-man does his job and not cares about his soul. Keep in mind: heart-men are serial killers. Everyone takes part in a crime and everyone knows it's a crime except for the mastermind. As immoral as it is, CeRue Manor saw it as a business and made sure to keep it that way, buying and selling human parts as commodities. Lonos had yet to prove it.

The Good Book teaches: 'For the love of money is a root of all kinds of evils'. It is through this craving that some wander away from their conscience and does not experience anything close to a sharp pang of guilt. They push God completely out of their life, and set their hope on the uncertainty of riches. These kinds of people always want more because greed strengthens their hands. Lonos saw Manor as someone insatiable.

CeRue Manor had the sixth sense to foresee the rich future. Now that Liberia was about to dip her foot in oil, he vowed to play a key role in it too. He was doing well, more than well. His wheeling and dealing concealed some of the biggest unlicensed business operations in Africa that made millions—the smuggling of diamonds, underage girls, and human organs. Since kickbacks and corruption turn a blind eye to regulations, smuggling paid exuberantly well, along with illegitimate private clubs.

If there was a place where people could meet with reasonable confidence that their deeds would not be exposed even in their world of ultra sophisticated matters of illegal, or even murderous, it was Manor's exclusive club, Le'Toit, (English translation-The Rooftop), a facility not for public. No one set foot in some areas and it was Manor who prescribed limits for his establishment. Even his trusted acquaintances went so far, and not further. Le'Toit was surrounded by hidden security cameras, and only Manor knew their locations.

'A fool's paradise', that's what Lynnette Vinton, aka Salvation Lady, calls the club, but services were premium all the way. "Satan is in the walls of that place," she often said.

Activities at Le'Toit was not limited to just a place where rich men met and drank, organized prostitution soared. Underage girls, barely teenage, were shipped in from neighboring counties to entertain these men. They had not come on their own, most being kidnapped. His assistant, an Ivorian native, handled all Manor's commodities, directing the routes of his precious freights—girls, human organs, drugs, diamonds, and weapons.

Inside the naughty housing of Le'Toit, amid the drinking, gambling and businessmen chatting their wheeling and dealing, the winding hall led to a place where a darker side of Manor's financial bloom lies, the top floor. Young girls are kept here to satisfy the men's lusts. The girls are forced to have sex with men for long hours, and are denied contact with anyone, family or others. Some were put into an international placement agency for mail-order brides. Human trafficking by unregulated placement agencies for maids, rather than prostitutes, was also a part of Manor's business. Demand for maids was increasing because in America and Europe, people would pay far less for what they would normally pay legal agencies for people to cook, clean, and look after their children.

Manor did not employ stupid people either, and his employees were compensated very well. Over half of his staff were imported into Liberia and they all had one thing in common; convicted criminal. He made sure all his well qualified employees had salaries bumped way higher than their counterparts, paying them far more than they'd earned any place else. His medical team was structured with an Asian doctor, an Indian surgeon, a Jamaican bartender, and a head waitress named Peaches.

Peaches had worked Las Vegas five years before coming to work for Manor. Wild as hell, she had spent more time in the backseat of cars than she did in the classroom, could drink any man under the table, and always had a purse full of pills. Other than her legal documents, passport or driver license, Peaches didn't need a last name.

Cheah Boatswain, a Monrovia city police officer, ran Manor's personal security force. Once a war lord, Boatswain was one of those who tried to make a holocaust out of Liberia all at once, fueling the senseless civil war with acts of violence beyond wordy description. Most remembered the mad killer, a short man with a shaven head and bushy beard. Though Boatswain had grown his hair and shaved his beard, people remembered him.

A civil war had been ignited because a few Liberian men turned war lords, set their minds on reversing peaceful living to war time so they could take ownership of things they did not want to work for. To rule you must serve, but their mixed-up instincts, and sneaking urge to power, permitted them to rule and get fancy cars and big houses they did not pay for. They turned from being family guards to become gun smugglers' customers who turned them into dogs. They sold drugs along with the country resources, like timbers and diamonds. They put guns and drugs into the hands of their sons and taught them to be rapists and murderers. The assaults on women were inconceivable, as if these men had never clinched to breasts that nourished them.

Today, lawless killings were in the past. But like every place in the world, crime still soared in Liberia.

ABOUT THE AUTHOR

Photo by Portia Langley

Ophelia S. Lewis is a poet, essayist, and creative writer. Heart Men is her first novel, and seventh book. She is the author of My Dear Liberia, which retells the enjoyable days in Liberia before the civil war. Her work appears in Diamonds & Pearls, a collection of poems published by the National Library of Poetry.

Especially interested in women and children's services, Lewis wrote two children's books in 2009; A is for Africa, a book where beginning readers learn about things in an African village as each letter is featured in a word on its own page with a photograph and The Good Manners Alphabet Book, which teaches young children good manners using the alphabets.

FOLLOW OPHELIA LEWIS ON
twitter: @ophie2020
website: www.ophelialewis.com
facebook: facebook.com/ophelia.lewis